This book is dedicated to my family

Thank you for ev

Also, thank you to the crew of
This voyage would never have I

Published by Thragoner Publishing, 2015

First edition, 2015

Pirates of the Blood Sea
Chapter 1: The Book

"All guns, fire!"

The command was yelled for effect more than anything, as none of the gunners on the deck below could hear it over the noise of the battle. Captain Crimson stood on a barrel with one foot on the ship's rail, a knife gripped between her teeth and her cutlass held high above her head. It inspired her pirates to fight harder when they saw their captain standing like a hero but Tom the cabin boy wondered how she managed to avoid being shot when she made such an obvious target. The roar of the cannons pulled him back to the battle; the side of the enemy ship shattered in a cloud of splintering wood and smoke. The most brutal pirates prepared to swing across the gap and start a boarding action, each holding a cutlass, club or knife but the crew of the merchant ship knew they were beaten and didn't want to die. Most of them threw their weapons down as the pirates swarmed across the gap; in less than a minute the merchantmen struck their flag, showing that they wanted to surrender. A few bloodthirsty pirates carried on slashing with their cutlasses or firing pistols but most soon set about tying up the prisoners and looking for valuables to steal.

The merchant captain tried to look brave but failed. Standing on the deck of the Crimson Firedrake surrounded by pirates with his hands tied behind his back, his head was held high but Tom could see him trembling. A few pirates were getting bored; some started to poke him with the tips of their cutlasses. Captain Crimson waited just long enough to raise the tension, then appeared on the poop deck.

"Now lads, don't be mistreating our fine guest. We owe him a debt of gratitude."

The pirates turned to stare as their captain jumped down the steps and wandered across to the captive.

"We owe him nothing."

The reply came from the first mate, Boulder, who delivered a stiff kick to the guts of the merchant captain as he said it. He was the exact opposite of his captain, a hulking brute of a man who lacked charisma but loved violence. The merchant captain folded in half and fell face down on the deck, gasping. Captain Crimson shook her head.

"Boulder, as usual your lack of manners shames us all. We owe this fine gentleman our thanks, for without him we would have no cargo to sell. So we will treat him as an honoured guest.

Turning to the bosun, she waved an arm.

"Mr Higgs, bring me wine for the captain!"

Higgs, a wiry man with a straggly beard, rushed off to find some wine. Captain Crimson continued with her performance, helping the merchant back to his feet.

"Of course, our new friend here will show how grateful he is for our generous hospitality by telling us where his gold is hidden."

The merchant captain spat on the floor.

"You attacked my ship and took my crew prisoner. Do you think I'll tell you how to finish your robbery?"

Captain Crimson smiled her most predatory smile.

"I've got a feeling you will, my friend. You see, all of your crew are tied up on what's left of your fine ship. Now, I've no use for your vessel. I have one of my own, and leaving yours behind will only give you a way of following me, so I've had all your barrels of gunpowder piled into the hold with a fuse set, ready to blow your ship to high heaven. It just so happens, the hold's where your crew are tied up for safekeeping. Now, I'd like to let you all go. I'm not a cruel woman after all. However, I am prone to fits of temper, and if someone refuses to tell me what I want to know..."

Captain Crimson shrugged her shoulders with a dramatic flourish.

"It's up to you. Do you have anything you want to tell me?"

The merchant captain swore. Captain Crimson pretended to be shocked.

"Such language from a gentleman. Sir, my crew are assembled and I'm not sure I want them to hear such words; they might start to repeat them, and then where would I be? Now, will you tell me what I want to know or do I get angry and send Mr Boulder to extinguish all traces of your unfortunate ship and crew?"

The merchant captain was a beaten man and he knew it. His shoulders slumped.

"The figurehead of my ship looks like she's made of wood, but she contains a secret compartment, lined with iron. If you push the left arm of the figurehead, her head will lift off. The gold is inside. May it burn a hole in your pockets and bring misery to every thieving dog aboard this vessel."

Captain Crimson performed a deep bow, sweeping her hat across her front with an extravagant flourish.

"My thanks. Now, Mr Higgs; hurry up with that wine for our guest."

Daniel closed the book. He was feeling tired now and while he wanted to read more about Captain Crimson and her crew, he knew that sleep would soon wrap its dark cloak around him and pull him into the otherworld of dreams. Putting the book down on his bedside table, he thought back to the afternoon and the trip to his uncle's shop; Uncle Alexander had owned the bookshop for as long as Daniel could remember. Daniel had always loved visiting his uncle in the shop. Sitting among the books, he would often find a quiet corner among the chaotic piles of ancient tomes and spend an hour escaping into the pages, reading stories of faraway places, brave heroes and cruel villains. For Daniel, a few hours spent with a book were the best way to travel to places he could reach only in his imagination.

Today, for a change, he had chosen an old book. Usually he managed to find something fairly new and exciting; while the shop specialised in old books, Uncle Alexander had to make a living and most of the people who came into the shop were looking for the latest bestseller. Children were no different, so there were often new books for children among the prizes on offer. However, this afternoon he had managed to exasperate his uncle by asking for something up to date about vampires.

"Honestly, boy. That's all I ever hear these days. It's enough to drive me to distraction, without my own family joining in. It's never the classic Dracula that they're after, is it? Oh no, it's these modern vampires with floppy hair, emotions and girlfriends. Go on, be off with you. Get out of my sight and find something worth reading!"

Daniel had seldom seen his uncle annoyed; he could be peculiar at times, prone to moments of grumpiness but he wasn't an angry man; his unexpected outburst sent Daniel running into the darkest places in the store room at the back of the shop. It only took a few minutes for Uncle Alexander to come and look for him, full of apologies and holding a sherbet lemon as a peace offering but by then, Daniel had found something to read. As he had crawled into the darkness between the stacks, his hand had rested on a thick and ancient book. He had ignored it at first, thinking it was just another dusty reference guide or fossilised textbook. However when he crawled over it his eye was drawn to the engraved image of a pirate flag on the cover and he picked it up, before crawling on into the gloom. Once he was out of sight, Daniel had examined his find. The title declared it to be "Pirates of the Blood Sea", written in gold above the flag. There were no other words on the thick, black cover so Daniel had opened the first page. The writing was small and hard to read in the darkness, so Daniel closed the book; he would read it later, when he could see more clearly.

His uncle had been interested by his choice, his bad mood forgotten as he turned the book over in his hands. His eyes sparkled as he looked at the cover.

"I thought that book had been lost forever. Where did you find it?"

Daniel had explained that it was at the back of the shop, lying among the piles of clutter. Uncle Alexander had suggested that he should start to read it that evening; if he enjoyed it, he could call back in the next day.

"I get the feeling you'll like this one, and if you do I've got something which might just add to the enjoyment. Call in after school and I'll tell you about it."

Daniel looked over at the book once more as he leaned across to turn off his bedside lamp. He could hear his mum shuffling about on the landing and knew that if she saw his light on, he'd be in trouble. The gold writing glinted in the dim light. Resisting the temptation to use a torch to read under his bedclothes, Daniel flipped the light switch. Sleep came rapidly, bringing dreams of a life on the high seas.

Daniel took the book with him to school the next day. He hoped to read some of it at lunchtime but everyone else wanted him to play football and wouldn't take no for an answer. After lunch, Daniel put his bag down on the classroom floor. The book slipped part of the way out, revealing the title. Daniel's friend George saw it.

"Is that your book? It looks ancient! Where did you get it?"

Daniel told his friend about finding the book at the back of his uncle's shop. George looked down at the book once more.

"Isn't it boring?"

Daniel stuffed the book back into his bag.

"It's good. I started it last night, I'm enjoying it so far."

George shook his head.

"Is it written in old fashioned language?"

Before Daniel could reply, the teacher called for silence and started the lesson.

The last lesson of the day on a Friday was a study time; pupils were expected to get on with their homework or read quietly to themselves. Daniel wasted no time in getting the book out and returning to the world of the pirates. However, there were no pirates at the start of the second chapter. Instead, it started with an admiral of the navy.

"It seems we have a problem with acts of piracy, gentlemen."

The Admiral strode up and down in front of the huge fireplace in his office. Several junior officers stood in front of him, all looking nervous. The Admiral was known to be a ferocious man when he was angry, and nothing angered him more than pirates sailing on his sea. One of the officers, feeling that he ought to respond to his superior, raised a hand.

"Many have been caught and brought to justice sir."

The Admiral spun to face the unfortunate underling.

"Many? By thunder, man! As long as one pirate remains at large, we are failing in our duty! Failing, do you hear me?"

It would be hard for the officer not to hear, as the Admiral shouted into his face from four inches away. Resuming his pacing, the Admiral continued his tirade.

"I received news just this morning that another merchant ship has been plundered and sunk. She was attacked within our waters by a gang of those thrice-be-damned rapscallions. Do you know what this means?"

Another officer provided the reply this time.

"More good men dead, sir."

The Admiral shook his head.

"On this occasion they were fortunate, gentlemen, and may all the powers of heaven be praised for that. Very few of the crew were slain in the rampage and the survivors escaped from the clutches of their captors. However, these men will now tell of how the navy failed in their duty of protection, gentlemen. These men will tell others who will spread the word among other crews until every sailor in these waters knows of your incompetence."

This was too much for the third officer, who interrupted.

"We're trying our best, sir."

The Admiral stopped walking. There was a deadly silence for a few seconds. When the Admiral spoke again it was with a quiet, dangerous voice.

"An attack on the king's navy is the same as an attack on the personage of the king himself. An attack on those under the protection of the king's navy is the same as an attack on the king's navy itself and therefore, an attack on those under the protection of the king's navy is the same as an attack on the king's navy itself and thus is the same as an attack on the king. Do you understand, gentlemen?"

The officers nodded, although none of them did. Fortunately for them, the Admiral carried on.

"Every time a pirate attacks a vessel in our waters, he is tweaking the nose of his majesty the king. Which of you will go and tell his majesty that his nose is being tweaked?"

The officers had, by this stage, realised that they were better off not speaking, especially if it involved telling the king about the tweaking of his nose. They waited in silence until the Admiral started talking once more.

"None of you. That duty falls to me, as the commanding officer in these waters. The king will be most displeased to learn of the latest affray in his waters and it will be hard for me

to explain it. Rest assured, gentlemen, should it go hard for me, it will go harder by far for each of you. Now you may dismiss."

The officers knew that this was a command. Each turned with a salute and marched from the room. The Admiral looked into the firelight and spoke under his breath, though there was nobody to hear him.

"I'll catch every one of you, by thunder. I'll see you all hanged if it takes me all my days on this earth."

Daniel was pulled back into the world of school by the bell to end the lesson. He put the book back into his bag; looking out of the window, he saw the puddles dancing as the raindrops landed with an irregular rhythm. He would have to run to Uncle Alexander's shop. Zipping the bag closed, Daniel pulled his coat over his head and set off running towards the school gate and freedom.

Uncle Alexander had put some newspaper on the floor. Daniel had to stand on it for a few minutes until he had finished dripping before his uncle would allow him in. Within a few minutes, the newspaper was soggy and while Daniel felt no drier, his uncle allowed him into the shop. The old bookseller seemed excited, leaning forward as Daniel approached the counter.

"Well? Did you start the book?"

Daniel nodded. Uncle Alexander was almost jumping with anticipation.

"What do you think of it?"

Daniel put his bag on the floor.

"It's good. I like it."

Uncle Alexander ran out from behind the counter and grabbed Daniel by the arm.

"You like it? My boy, that's a terrible, bland understatement! One likes a packet of crisps or an amusing joke. This book is magnificent; to describe it as merely "good" is a terrible insult!"

Daniel wondered why his uncle was acting so strangely. He tried to sound more enthusiastic.

"Sorry uncle. I really like it. I read it last night until I fell asleep. Captain Crimson is wonderful."

Uncle Alexander released Daniel's arm. Daniel was pleased as his uncle had been gripping it very hard.

"That's a bit better, although I still think you're doing the book a disservice. You should watch out for Captain Crimson too; she is a pirate after all."

Daniel looked up at his uncle.

"Are you saying that she turns out to be a baddie?"

Uncle Alexander seemed to be surprised by the question; he struggled to answer, which surprised Daniel. Eventually he took a breath and said

"I think it's best if you just read the book and get to know her for yourself. Now as I promised, I have something that may help make it all more real for you. Follow me."

Before Daniel could ask him anything else, his uncle dashed off towards the store room at the back of the shop.

Uncle Alexander picked up a wooden box from a table in the store room. Daniel looked at it; it was old and covered in a layer of dust. He wondered what it could be, and how it connected to the book. He could see no obvious clues, so he asked his uncle directly;

"What's in the box?"

His uncle's eyes shone as he replied.

"It's a map."

Chapter 2: The Map

Daniel opened the box. Inside was a rolled up piece of parchment and three pins, each with a small model of a human head on top. Putting the box down, Daniel unfurled the parchment. It was, as his uncle had said, a map. It was faded and yellow with age, crossed with lines and measurements. It was labelled "The Blood Sea" and showed a coastline dotted with islands. Several were named; Daniel saw Stone Island, Steamhead Island, Wick Island and Longneck Island, with several smaller islands towards the south such as Goose Rock and Doom Atoll. He looked up at his uncle.

"Is this the map of the place where the pirates live?"

Uncle Alexander nodded.

"It is."

Daniel grinned.

"Cool."

He rolled the map up, then reached across to pick up the box, moving a pile of papers from one of the wooden chairs that had been in the storeroom for as long as he could remember. Daniel checked the seat then sat down, mindful of splinters. His uncle produced two cups of tea from somewhere and sat down next to him.

"Spread the map out."

Daniel did as he was asked. Clearing a small coffee table with a swipe of his arm, Uncle Alexander used the tea cups to hold the corners down.

"Now, there are some things you need to know before you use this map."

Daniel, who was trying to take a sip of tea without the map curling up, replied with some questions

"Use the map? What for? How?"

Uncle Alexander used his elbow to pin the map while he had a sip of tea.

"All in good time. First, I will tell you some important things that you must know."

Daniel leaned forward as his uncle explained.

"The first thing I want you to promise is that you will keep the map safe. It is very old and needs to be treated carefully."

Daniel interrupted with a question.

"Where did it come from?"

His uncle waved the question away with his arm

"Don't distract me, Daniel. You must listen and learn, it is important. Now as I said, the map will help you to see more of the world of pirates but you must use it carefully. Never get the map out when other people are around; last thing before you go to bed is best, when you won't be interrupted."

Daniel wanted to ask why but didn't dare. Truthfully, he found his uncle a bit strange at times like this and he felt it would be rude to interrupt again. Uncle Alexander continued

"Most important is this; in the interests of safety, you must never place a map pin into the sea. Always put them into land. I suggest you start at Port St David, it's the naval capital; always a good place to begin. Any questions?"

Daniel shook his head. He waited for a few seconds, expecting his uncle to continue but instead he sipped his tea and stayed quiet. Daniel looked at him.

"I don't understand what I'm supposed to do. Are you going to tell me what I need to do to use it, or even what I'm using the map for?"

Uncle Alexander started to roll up the map and put it into the box.

"What? Oh yes. You use it to find out more about the world of the pirates."

Daniel was confused.

"I know, you said that before. How do I use it? What does it do?"

Uncle Alexander picked up one of the pins from the box. He reached forward and pulled a hair from Daniel's head. Daniel yelled, more in shock than pain. Ignoring him, his uncle tied the hair around one of the pins.

You simply take this pin and stick it in the map. Now, you run along home. It's getting late and I have to close the shop."

Daniel was still confused as his uncle bustled him out into the cold evening, holding the precious map box.

The rain had given way to a light breeze; twilight cast long shadows across the playground as Daniel took the short cut home. Deep in thought, he didn't notice that there were three people hanging around near the swings until he was almost there; two were sitting on the swings with another one leaning on the frame. Daniel knew who they were as soon as he saw them. Barry, Bill and Owen were a bit older than Daniel, in the same school year but old enough to be bigger and stronger. Sometimes they were friendly to Daniel but more often they weren't. This was one of those occasions.

"Oi, bookworm. What've you got there?"

Barry stood up from the swing and walked forward as he saw Daniel, his two companions falling into line next to him. Daniel considered running but that would mean walking the long way home and besides, he didn't want to look weak to the three; that would mean a tough time at school next day. He replied, forcing himself to sound casual.

"Nothing. Just my school things."

Bill, the tallest of the three, sneered.

"You're late going home. Isn't it past your bedtime?"

All three laughed. Daniel pretended to laugh too, walking on and hoping that he could get past them without them bothering him. Barry spotted his plan and stepped in front of him.

"That box isn't from school. What is it?"

Daniel thought about making up a story but decided that the truth would do just as well.

"It's a box that my uncle gave me."

Owen, who had stepped behind Daniel, grabbed the box out of his hand. Daniel spun around and tried to take it back but Owen was too fast and too strong. He held the box in the air, out of reach.

"Your weird uncle who runs the bookshop?"

Daniel didn't answer. He tried to grab his box back but Owen shoved him away, then threw it to Bill.

"What's inside, then? Let's have a look."

"Nothing interesting. It's just an old box. Let me have it back, please."

Daniel made a desperate attempt to grab the box but Barry stopped him as Bill opened it and pulled out the map.

"Oo, look, a treasure map. Has your mad uncle been burying treasure?"

He threw the map and box to Owen, who unrolled the map.

"Isn't it pretty? Did Uncle Nutter draw it for you?"

Daniel was getting angry; he didn't like hearing his family insulted. He ran across to Owen.

"Just give it back."

He shoved Owen, who stumbled backwards and dropped the box. Owen snarled at him.

"You little turd."

Barry slapped Daniel on the back of the head.

"Feeling brave? Want a fight, do you?"

Owen stepped forward, swinging a punch towards Daniel's head. Daniel ducked and avoided the blow but Bill pushed him while he was off balance. Daniel stumbled towards the twisted remains of an iron fence which had once bordered the playground. He recovered his balance and glanced back. Owen was still holding the map and was advancing towards him. Daniel tried to grab it again but missed. Owen held it up in front of him, using both hands.

"Shall I rip it in half?"

"No!"

Daniel's yell of despair brought laughter from the trio. Owen threw the map on the floor and shoved Daniel hard, sending him sprawling over the wrecked fence into the mud. Daniel felt cold wetness spreading through the seat of his trousers. He tried to scramble to his feet but slipped down again, his palms slipping in the dirt. Barry stepped forward, standing over the box and map. He pointed and laughed.

"Look, the bookworm's in the mud where he belongs. Feel at home there, worm?"

Daniel climbed to his feet, angry. He ran forward to Barry and hit him as hard as he could. The blow caught Barry on the arm and had no obvious effect other than to make Barry retaliate. He punched Daniel hard in the stomach, knocking the wind out of him and sending him to the floor, gasping. Tears sprang to his eyes but he was determined not to cry. He tried to stand but Owen gave him a kick, sending him sprawling on the floor again. Bill shouted across.

"Go on worm, run back to your mad uncle."

Owen kicked the box, sending it bouncing across the floor.

"You can give him this back, if he wants it."

With that, the three of them walked away, Owen treading on the map as he left. Daniel fought to get his breathing under control. The physical pain hurt but far worse was the loneliness, the feeling that nobody in the world cared, that nobody would help him. Fighting back the tears, Daniel wiped his muddy hands on the grass then picked up the map. There was a dirty footprint on the back and some mud stains on the front; Daniel could picture Uncle Alexander's disappointed face as he looked at the ruined map. Hoping that the damage could be repaired, he put it back in the box and set off into the gloom towards his home.

Daniel snuck in through the back door, sneaking upstairs to hide his filthy state from his mum. Only once he had put his clothes into the washing basket and changed into jeans and a T shirt did he get the map out. The footprint was planted across the middle and there were other mud stains in a few places. After he had closed the door, Daniel pinned the map to his bedside table with a model boat and a coffee mug then used a damp sponge to remove the worst of the mud. To his great relief, the map itself wasn't ripped and after cleaning, the mud stains were less noticeable among the marks of age on the map; it looked less battered than he was. Leaving it to dry and praying it wouldn't look too bad, Daniel got the book out and began to read, hoping to take his mind off his bruises and aches.

The Crimson Firedrake had been in Blackrum harbour for no more than two hours but most of the crew were at the Inn of the She Wolf and were already drunk. Captain Crimson sat with a few trusted companions at a table in the corner of the tavern. Boulder was among them; the mirthless giant never drank and while his company wasn't much fun, he made a good bodyguard. The other members of the inner circle were old hands, pirates who had sailed with Captain Crimson for years. There was only one new face with them; for the first time, Tom was included among the Captain's inner circle. He had no idea what had made the Captain decide to involve him and he sat in silence as the others discussed their plans.

"Once we've unloaded and sold our plunder, I say we head back to open water and find a rich merchant ship. We need a good payday."

Captain Crimson shook her head.

"There's no bigger gambler than me, you all know that. The thing is, when I gamble I like to win and right now there are too many pirates losing that gamble in deep waters."

Pablo Estoril, a wiry man in a headscarf, spoke from the other end of the table.

"You think we should stick to the safe places? Stay in the shallows like little children and live off scraps? A pirate's life is one long risk."

Captain Crimson took a drink of wine.

"Pablo, I don't like the situation any more than you do but I like the Firedrake and want to keep her. Between the navy on the one hand and Captain Ironskull on the other, the risk is too big."

There were murmurings of discontent around the table but they were against Captain Ironskull, not their own captain. Pablo stood up and stabbed a dagger into the table.

"It's not right, what Ironskull's doing. We should do something."

Captain Crimson leaned back.

"What do you suggest? Have you got a plan?"

One of the other crew members answered, a round bellied man known as Boar.

"No pirate should attack another pirate vessel in open water. We fight him, that's the plan."

Several of his shipmates nodded and mumbled agreement. Captain Crimson applauded with sarcastic slowness.

"Well done, a magnificent plan. I take my hat off to you."

She did exactly this, putting it on the table with a sweep of her arm as she stood up.

"Now tell me, what will stop Captain Ironskull treating us exactly the same way he's treated everyone else he's fought? The few survivors of those battles have told us why we can't beat him. You've all heard the tales; he captains a ship of iron, powered by steam and sorcery. Cannonballs bounce off the hull and the ship attacks from nowhere and vanishes like the fog, leaving nothing but blood and fire behind him. Even the navy is wary of him. Tell me, how do you suggest we defeat a foe like that?"

Tom leapt to his feet.

"You're Captain Crimson, captain of the Crimson Firedrake! You're one of the most feared pirates on the Blood Sea! You've escaped from the navy five times. You've stolen the King's treasure ship from the royal harbour. You can do anything. Why don't you make one of your plans and outwit him like you have everyone else?"

Captain Crimson smiled at him.

"Tom, I knew there was a reason I wanted you here."

She placed a foot on the chair, handed Tom a flagon and addressed her crew.

"Tom is right. We will find a way to defeat him and make him pay for attacking his fellow pirates. However, I'll need time to think of the perfect plan, so for a while we'll keep a low profile. A few weeks are all it'll take, and then I'll make you all famous as the crew that beat the unbeatable Captain Ironskull. What say you all?"

"Aye!"

While everyone lifted their ale and joined in the shout, there was more than one pair of mutinous eyes among those sitting around the table.

Daniel put his bookmark back into the book, then put the book onto the table next to the map. The edges of the map were still moist but the centre was dry and much of the mud was gone; he would need to clean it more in the morning but his sense of despair lifted a little at the improvement. Daniel thought about going downstairs but the map pins in the box caught his eye. Without quite knowing why, he picked up the pin with his hair tied to it. Remembering the warning his uncle had given, he closed the door with his foot before turning his attention to the map. Port St David was easily found, in the centre of the coastline. However, Daniel's attention was drawn to Stone Island in the south eastern corner of the map. Blackrum was on the east of the island. Daniel remembered his uncle's words;

"You use it to find out more about the world of the pirates."

The town where Captain Crimson had docked sounded far more exciting than the respectable Port St David so Daniel plunged his pin into the town.

Daniel felt as if he had just woken up. Hard stones pressed into his back. His shoulders ached and pain like lightning flashed across his head with every movement. The sun blazed overhead, hurting his eyes. Rolling to his side to get some shade on his face, Daniel looked up; above him was an old fashioned tavern with a wooden sign creaking in the breeze. Daniel had to rub his eyes and look again; the sign showed a grey wolf head howling at the moon. Underneath, the tavern name was written:

"The Inn of the She Wolf".

Chapter 3: The Crew

Daniel stared at the tavern sign. He mumbled to himself

"Am I dreaming?"

A hand hauled him up from the gutter by his collar.

"You're not dreaming boy. It's going to be more like a nightmare for you once the captain gets her hands on you."

Daniel looked over his shoulder at the person holding him. It was a pirate with a scraggly beard, wearing a headscarf. Daniel remembered chapter one of the book. Although he could hardly believe it, he found himself asking the pirate his name;

"Are you Higgs?"

The bosun looked at him as if he was mad.

"You know I am. Have you been fighting? Has someone knocked you on the head?"

Daniel didn't answer; he was too stunned to say anything. He allowed himself to be led along the harbour until they reached a ship, tied up at the end of a short jetty; her nameplate, as Daniel expected, named her "The Crimson Firedrake". An impressive dragon's head jutted from the front of the vessel as a figurehead, painted in red with blazing orange eyes. As they reached the ship, a young pirate stepped onto the gangplank, challenging them.

"Who goes there?"

Higgs' reply was to give him a slap on the back of the head as they shoved past onto the ship. Within a few seconds, a tall woman in a red lined tailcoat strode across the deck towards them; Daniel knew who it was without having to be told; she walked as if she owned the deck. Which, Daniel realised, she did. There was one thing about her that he hadn't anticipated; without meaning to, he spoke out loud.

"Ginger hair."

Captain Crimson raised an eyebrow.

"That's flame red hair as I've told you many times, you cheeky young whippersnapper. There aren't many captains who would put up with such insubordination; most would have you keelhauled for speaking to your fearless leader in such a disrespectful manner. Anyway, enough jabbering. You finally decided to come back to us, did you Tom?"

Daniel was confused.

"Tom?"

Higgs jerked him forward by the collar, hurting his neck and causing him to choke.

"I think he's been on the grog, or he's been hit on the head. He didn't know who I was when I found him."

Captain Crimson looked at him.

"He doesn't look injured so it must be the grog. Take him below, he can sleep it off. We've got more important things to worry about. I'll deal with him later."

With that, Daniel was lifted off his feet and hauled below decks.

There was no space below. Higgs had to duck so that he didn't hit his head on the ceiling. After a few paces, he dumped Daniel down like a sack of potatoes and shoved him forward.

"You can walk from here."

Daniel stumbled forward and tripped over a coil of rope; his head missed a cannon by inches. He scrambled to his hands and knees; Higgs had already returned above deck. A voice squeaked out of the darkness.

"Are you alright, Tom?"

Daniel looked around, but couldn't see anyone. He assumed the voice was talking to him; everyone seemed to think he was Tom the cabin boy and he didn't feel like arguing; he needed to work out what had happened, how he had ended up inside the book. A moment of panic hit him like cold water in the face; what if he couldn't get home? The voice brought him back from his worry;

"Can you hear me?"

Daniel's eyes were adjusting to the dark but he still couldn't see the owner of the voice.

"I can but I can't see you."

A head popped up from behind a cannon. It displayed the type of smile that would be most at home on the face of a young child although the head was balding, grey haired and wrinkled.

"Here I am."

Daniel smiled.

"Why are you hiding there?"

"I'm avoiding work, of course. I'm supposed to be part of the deck swabbing team but it's far too nice a day to be pushing a mop around so I'm down here in the dark. Most of the crew still think I'm ashore, so I'll pretend to come back from the town in an hour or so and join in for the last little bit. That way, I'll be working when they hand out the grog which means I'll get my share."

Daniel sat down on a barrel. The old man jumped out from behind the cannon and landed next to him. He was agile for his age, dressed in a baggy pair of trousers and a colourful shirt. Daniel decided that he was friendly and that he wouldn't be offended if he was asked his name.

"I'm really sorry; I've been a bit confused today. I've forgotten your name."

The old man laughed.

"Forgotten? If you're going to forget something you have to know it first. You've never known my name, so you couldn't forget it even if you tried."

Daniel was puzzled.

"Haven't I?"

The old man smiled at him.

"No, you haven't. In fact, you don't know any of us. You've never been on board this ship before, have you?"

He paused for a few seconds before continuing,

"Have you, Tom?"

The old man looked him in the eyes as he said the name "Tom". His face seemed older all of a sudden, older and wiser. Daniel felt the panic rising inside him.

"How do you know? You won't…"

The old man put a hand on his shoulder and his friendly manner came back like the sun from behind a cloud.

"Don't panic, boy, I'm not going to tell anyone. I don't want to see a lad like you in trouble. I'm more interested in where you've come from though, since you're clearly not part of the crew, however much you look like the cabin boy. As for how I know, I could tell you that but only if you're a good boy."

The man winked and pulled up a storage chest.

"Now, tell me who you are, where you've come from and how you got here. Are you a water spirit or something? A changeling? Should we have you run through with silver and locked in a lead lined chest, sunk to the bottom of the sea and imprisoned for all time?"

Daniel didn't like the sound of that. He told his tale to the old man, including the part about the book and the map. He didn't expect his companion to believe him but to his surprise, the old man just nodded.

"A dreamwalker, how interesting. It's been a while since we had one of those."

Daniel was confused.

"A what? I'm not dreaming, am I? I can't be."

The man jumped onto the barrel of the cannon, one leg either side like an iron horse.

"No, you don't have to be dreaming to dreamwalk. It's our name for someone who travels between the worlds. It's been a long time since someone visited us that way. I've often wondered how it would feel to do it but I've never managed it however hard I've tried."

Daniel shrugged.

"If I can travel this way, there might be a way for you to come back with me."

The man shook his head.

"Not that I know of, and if anyone would know, I would."

Daniel walked towards the cannon. Before he got there, the old man slid down backwards, turning a backflip at the bottom to land on his feet. Daniel watched in amazement.

"How do you know all this?"

He hesitated for a second.

"Who are you?"

The old man rubbed his chin.

"You seem like a good lad, so I'll tell you a few things. My name, as I'm known by the sailors on this ship, is Skop Groggen. That's not my real name; I'm not planning to tell you or anyone else what that is as names have power. As for what I am, the sailors on this ship call me a Sea Wizard. Most pirates keep one aboard; we make sure they don't do anything dangerously unlucky, we read the signs in the sky, predict the weather, get rid of evil spirits, that sort of thing."

Daniel looked at the old man. It all seemed highly unlikely but then, so did waking up inside the world of a book. He had a sudden thought.

"Why haven't I read about you in the book?"

Skop Groggen looked surprised.

"I'm not in the book? I must change that…"

He was interrupted as a giant man squeezed himself down the steps. To Daniel it seemed he was all beard and belly. He roared when he saw them, pointing a sausage of a finger at Skop Groggen.

"Here you are, you lazy old windbag. Wasting time with the cabin boy when you should be on deck!"

Skop jumped behind the cannon where the giant couldn't reach him. Daniel stepped out of the way as the huge sailor's bulk rumbled past him like an avalanche. Skop dodged a meaty fist and skipped out behind the giant.

"There's more than enough people to do the deck swabbing. I'll join in once I've finished talking to the boy. I tell you what, Bear; you can do my share while you're waiting for me. It's the best thing for a foam witted bilge brain like you."

Bear roared once more and tried to turn to grab Skop but the narrow space made turning impossible. He settled for grabbing Daniel, lifting him up and tucking him under one arm.

"You'll pay for that once I get my hands on you."

Skop laughed and jumped back behind the cannon.

"Just go and do the swabbing like a good Bear."

Bear threw Daniel towards the steps, then yelled back towards Skop.

"No. it's captain's orders, you get up on deck now. Swabbing can wait; we need you on deck for a crew meeting. We're taking this ship to war."

The rest of the crew was already assembled when Daniel and Skop arrived. The atmosphere was tense. Two groups had formed and were facing each other with half the crew in each. In the middle, Captain Crimson was talking to two men; one was thin and wiry, the other had a large belly. Daniel picked up the conversation as he was shoved forward.

"…I won't give away the lives of good men just because you can't wait a few weeks, Pablo."

The smaller of the men replied with feeling.

"We won't stand by and wait for you to think of a plan which will never come. We've been waiting days and you've done nothing, not even left port for some simple looting. The crew have voted and these men want to attack. That's what we're going to do, whatever you say."

Captain Crimson stood her ground.

"If you're going to do that, you need your captain to order it or you need to win the vote. Has there been a count?"

The man with the belly nodded.

"Aye, it's come out even so far, half for attacking and half for waiting. We need these two to vote and it's done."

He motioned towards Bear and Daniel.

"You're with me, Bear. You know that."

Bear walked across the deck and stood with the round bellied Boar.

"Now we're winning by one vote. Boy, come over here!"

Captain Crimson shrugged.

"Bear and Boar, together as always. No surprises there. So it comes down to you, Tom. Which way will you vote?"

Daniel felt the eyes of the crew upon him, waiting for his decision. Not daring to look Bear in the eye, he stepped towards Captain Crimson.

"I'm with you, Captain."

Captain Crimson smiled.

"Sensible lad. So, it's still an even split. As you all know, when that happens, the captain takes the deciding vote…"

Before she could complete her sentence, another voice piped up from the hatch. It was Skop Groggen.

"I haven't voted yet."

The old wizard hopped out of the hatch and danced across the deck towards them. Boar looked at him in disgust.

"Madmen and idiots don't get to vote."

"Says who?"

Skop Groggen walked up to the large duo, hands in pockets. He didn't look worried, even though there were two of them and both were much bigger than him. Boar replied to his question.

"It's pirate rules."

Captain Crimson held up her hand to silence them.

"I'm the captain and I decide who votes. That's also in the pirate rules, in case you'd forgotten and I see no reason for keeping Skop Groggen out of the vote."

Skop performed a theatrical bow. For a moment, it seemed that Boar might punch him. The small man next to him spat out a response.

"Vote then, you old fool and get back to your nonsense and your gibbering. Leave the proper fighting to decent pirates and go back to telling fairy-tales to small boys and gullible simpletons."

Skop pretended to be upset.

"Oh, Pablo. You wound me with your cruel words. You should listen more and talk less, then everyone would hear less of your dull witted droning and more of my wisdom."

Pablo drew a knife. Captain Crimson drew her sword.

"There will be no fighting. None of you will lay a hand on my Sea Wizard and we will finish the vote. Skop Groggen, say what you have to say and cast your vote."

Pablo lowered his knife but didn't put it away. Skop Groggen sat on the floor, cross legged.

"What I have to say is this; better one volunteer than ten pressed men."

Boar looked down at him.

"What's that supposed to mean?"

Skop spoke slowly, as if addressing a small child.

"A pressed man is one who is kidnapped by a press gang and forced to sail on a ship even though he doesn't want to…"

Boar roared at him.

"I know what a pressed man is! I want to know why you said that and what your vote is. Stop wasting our time."

Skop Groggen stood.

"I mean this; each of us should be free to take whatever course of action he, or indeed she, sees fit."

He turned to acknowledge his Captain, who nodded and waved for him to continue.

"We are split on this decision. Whatever happens, half of the crew will be unhappy. So I say that those who want to fight should go; choose a captain, leave the Firedrake, find a ship and go. Those who trust Captain Crimson should stay."

Captain Crimson leaned on the tip of her sword.

"Your words change nothing. Which way will you vote?"

"I don't think I need to vote. Those who want to go should go whether I vote or not. When it comes to staying or leaving, I think I'll stay here with Captain Crimson. She seems a little more receptive to my wise advice."

Pablo finally put his knife away.

"You heard the fool. Who is coming with us, to fight?"

Most of those who had voted to fight raised their hands and cheered. One or two of the younger men in the middle looked nervous; Bear loomed over them.

"Hands up boys. Come with us and we'll take the fight to Captain Ironskull."

"I'm not sure…"

A blonde lad, nervous and thin, seemed to be wavering. Captain Crimson offered him her hand.

"John, you make whatever decision you feel is best. You're still part of my crew, you can stay if you want to."

"He doesn't want to. You want to come with us, don't you John?"

Boar stared hard at young John.

"Don't you John?"

John looked at Boar, then back at his captain, then back to Boar. After a few seconds, he nodded.

"I'll fight."

With a cheer, Boar and his crew turned and headed for the gangplank. Captain Crimson stood and watched as they left the ship.

"Well, Skop, you've caused me no end of trouble today. I'm going to need a new crew now."

Skop Groggen also watched as the last of the men left the ship in an excited huddle.

"Only half a crew, if we're being picky. Besides, keeping them would only have led to trouble in the long run. You know that."

Captain Crimson sighed.

"You're right, as usual. It'll take a while to find men good enough to replace them, especially with my reputation as the greatest pirate in the Blood Sea fading like smoke on the wind. Perhaps some of them will change their minds and come back to us in a few days."

Skop Groggen shook his head.

"You won't see any of them again. They're going to pick a fight they can't win. None of those men will be alive by this time tomorrow."

Chapter 4: Captain Ironskull

Daniel woke up. He was lying on his back, on his bed. A glance at the clock and the light streaming through the curtains showed that the night had passed; it was early morning. What had happened? He tried to think through the brain fog of first waking, trying to remember.

The events on the ship came back to him. He remembered Skop Groggen, the meeting on board ship and half the crew leaving; what had happened after that? He had asked about getting home, he remembered that much. Skop had been very calm about it all, saying that he would go back sooner or later.

"Don't worry" he had said,

"You got here, so you'll get back. Have some sleep and the answer may become clear, the morning is wiser than the evening."

Daniel had given up trying to get any sense out of him and had found an unoccupied hammock. The rocking of the boat had been very relaxing; the next thing he knew, he was here in his bed.

Had it been a dream? It felt more vivid than any dream, more real. Daniel glanced across to the table where he had put the map. It was exactly where he had left it but when he looked more closely, he saw that his pin was no longer stuck into the map but had been put back in the box. Rolling to his right, he picked up the book. His bookmark had moved; now it was on an unread passage about the Navy.

The officer knocked on the door, fiddling with his buckle as he did so. A meeting with The Admiral always made him nervous; neatness and attention to detail were two of the areas where one had to be most careful. Appearing before The Admiral with so much as a button out of place would put him in a foul temper and make the meeting all the more difficult.

A few seconds passed before a voice barked the command;

"Enter!"

The officer turned the handle, his hand feeling as if he had been lying on it for half an hour. He debated in his own mind how wide he should open the door; too wide would appear forward and rude. Humility would be better, so he opened it just a crack and squeezed in. His sword hilt caught on the doorknob which then tangled in his sword belt with a loud clatter. The officer panicked; in his attempt to free his belt, his trousers came undone; haste made him clumsy and in attempting to do up his trousers, his finger got stuck in the button hole. The Admiral regarded him during this performance.

"Tell me, do you consider it appropriate to remove your trousers in order to greet a superior officer? Do you think such a greeting is in line with Naval protocol?"

The officer removed his finger from the button hole as if stung, then grabbed at his belt loops as his trousers began to slip down. His sword swung back and forth like a pendulum.

"No sir. I can assure you that I am merely attempting to remedy an accidental slippage in my uniform. I would never consider undressing myself in front of a superior officer, sir."

The Admiral ignored the continued trouser fumbling and turned to the issue in hand.

"I assume you have come to provide me with a report on our on-going campaign against the pirate menace and that your lack of appropriate dress is as a result of your haste to bring me your report. You shall therefore deliver your report with equal haste, as I am a busy man and have vital duties to attend to. I trust there has been significant success since your last report?"

The officer cleared his throat.

"There have been some developments, sir."

The Admiral remained as still as stone.

"Do the developments involve the sinking of every pirate vessel in these waters and the capture of every significant pirate captain in order that they might face good Naval justice?"

The officer shook his head.

"No sir…"

The Admiral interrupted.

"Then your work is not yet completed. Make your report as fast as you are able and return to your duty. While a single pirate remains at large to trouble the decent people that sail upon the waters for which we have responsibility, we do not have time to waste in idle chatter or removing our trousers in the presence of our superiors. Speak with alacrity and waste no words in verbose prattle, for we have not the time to accommodate such indulgences."

The officer tightened his grip on his belt.

"Yes sir. Our agents have been observing the activities of the pirates in Blackrum Port. It appears that half of Captain Crimson's crew have declared themselves independent of the female rogue and have set off to pick a fight with Captain Ironskull. The most likely outcome is that their vessel will be burned to the waterline and they will be killed or captured. However, this tells us one thing of great importance."

The Admiral nodded.

"They have not previously fought amongst themselves, unless I am mistaken."

The Admiral's tone suggested that he could not possibly be mistaken. The officer was wise enough to agree.

"Absolutely, sir. They seem to operate according to a set of rules; they may be bloodthirsty ne'er-do-wells but they aren't completely chaotic. This is the first time we have seen them set out to fight one another in anything bigger than a bar room brawl."

"Why does this concern us?"

The officer answered the question in a burst of enthusiasm, his confidence building as he spoke.

"If they have started to engage in open sea battles against one another, it may be a situation which we can use to help us bring them all to justice. My agents will continue to observe and gather information about what is happening and why. If nothing else, several of the pirates will be eliminated in the fighting. This will make our task all the easier."

The Admiral's face returned to its usual mask of steel.

"Then I will expect it to be completed all the sooner. Now you may dismiss and make sure that your trousers are hoisted above half-mast at all times."

Daniel put the book down while he drank a glass of water. Flicking back a few pages to the previous chapter confirmed everything that he had been through since he put the pin into the map; it was all there in black and white on the pages. He knew that he hadn't read it the previous evening. Turning to the bookmarked page once more, Daniel saw that the coming section dealt with Boar and Bear's attack on Captain Ironskull. Fearing the worst, he read on with growing dread.

"They come closer, sir."

The pirate turned to face his captain. He had been looking through a brass viewing tube which screwed directly into his mechanical eye; as it was attached to the wall of the ship, turning round took some time. Captain Ironskull waited with a patience that showed extreme confidence. The eerie green light below decks combined with the rusted walls and constant dripping of water to create the appearance of an ancient metal cave. The master of the cave spoke, his voice deep and resonating.

"Let them come. We have nothing to fear from their cannons."

The crew laughed. Each of them had several body parts which had been exchanged for mechanical replacements; one had a leg which was operated by a metal piston, another had an arm which was now a semi-automatic pistol, powered by compressed gas and gunpowder. However, none could match their captain for mechanisation; at first glance, he appeared to be more machine than man. His head, which gave him his name, was now a mixture of helmet and shaven head, the iron of the helmet riveted directly into the huge pirate's skull. His left eye was now an extending brass telescope, his right ear had been replaced by a copper box and an aerial. His body, solid and large as a barrel, was an iron construction which now showed signs of rust and discolouring. His legs looked like they were made from scaffolding but it was his arm which drew the attention; it was a complex mechanical contraption, powered by cogwheels and steam. This operated a hand which could be changed for a variety of weapons and implements; currently, a huge three fingered claw was screwed into the wrist socket. A chimney sprouted from his shoulder. It belched grey steam into the chamber inside the iron ship, increasing the gloom.

The first mate, a metal masked monster of a man responded to his captain.

"Do we open fire ourselves, Captain? They are coming into range of the aft turret cannon."

"Open fire but don't sink them. I want their rudder disabled and their masts taken down."

Several crewmembers left to fulfil this command. The captain faced those who remained.

"Let them have their moment of hope. They may think that they will escape but once we have what we want, we send them all to sleep with the fishes."

The metal cavern echoed to the sound of cruel laughter as the crew finished preparing for slaughter.

"We haven't even dented them, Captain!"

John called in desperation to Boar, the newly elected captain of the Scourge of Iron. Boar swore and turned to his first mate, Bear.

"What do you think we should do?"

Bear shrugged his mountainous shoulders.

"Prepare to repel boarders?"

Boar slapped his hand onto the rail in frustration as another volley of cannonballs slammed into the side of their metal enemy, causing a loud noise but nothing else.

"Anything else?"

Bear looked across the water at the iron vessel closing in on them.

"I can't think of anything. Your plan doesn't seem to have worked..."

He paused for a few seconds, before adding

"Captain."

Boar snapped at his large partner.

"What plan?"

"Your plan to buy a small, fast ship with accurate cannons, then hunt Captain Ironskull down."

Boar's anger and frustration boiled over as he rounded on Bear.

"It was your plan too, in case you've forgotten and it all went wrong when they came out of nowhere to attack us. Speed should've kept us away from their cannons. How could I know they'd put turrets on a ship?"

Bear shouted back.

"What, did you think everyone else was just unlucky? That we could just sail up and sink them? I thought you had a better plan than just speed."

The argument raged like the cannon fire all around them. Boar yelled his reply.

"My plan should've worked but that ship's in league with evil. Speed and accuracy won't help if your enemy can appear behind you like a wraith and floating iron just isn't natural. Blaming me won't help us win this battle. What you need to do is…"

A roar of cannon fire cut him off, as the turret on the front of the iron ship spat fire and death towards them. Boar jumped backwards as the stern took the brunt of the impact, shards and splinters flying in all directions; picking himself up from the deck, Boar saw that Bear was lying face down, not moving. Blood pooled around his head. Boar cursed again, then turned to shout orders to his crew;

"Take weapons and stand fast boys! Show no mercy and offer no quarter, for you know you'll receive none! Prepare to fight for your lives!"

The fight was swift and bloody. The Scourge of Iron's rudder was shot away by the cannon blast; without it, Captain Ironskull was able to stay out of range of the enemy cannons and keep circling, firing his own turrets into the sitting target. Within minutes, most of Boar's crew were dead or swimming for their lives while their ship burned; when Captain Ironskull's men boarded, they found very few alive and ready to fight.

Captain Ironskull walked along the burning deck, the fire making his iron parts glow red and orange like a creature from the deepest infernal pit. His steam powered claw had been replaced with a buzzing chain blade, all the better for close quarter fighting although he had needed to do very little of that.

"Captain, over here."

A pirate with a metal plate over one eye called to his captain, who turned to face him.

"You have a live one?"

"Aye sir!"

John groaned. He had been knocked out during the fighting when a section of the mast had knocked him on the head as it was blasted apart. The metal plated face was not a welcome sight as he came to and neither were Captain Ironskull's words;

"Bring him aboard. Then burn this ship."

John pulled against the chains holding him but it was useless; they were an inch thick and fastened to the structure of the ship itself. Captain Ironskull stood in front of him, his bladed hand whirring.

"This is the last time I'll ask, sailor. What does Captain Crimson have planned?"

Captain Ironskull raised the blade alarmingly close to John's face. He tried to pull away, but the chains held him fast.

"Ok, I'll tell you what I know."

"Be swift."

Captain Ironskull revved his blade, sending a burst of steam into the air from the pipes on his shoulder. John babbled his answer as fast as he could.

"She's keeping to the waters around Blackrum at the moment, picking on easy targets. She had no immediate plans to come after you and will probably take even longer now as she needs a new crew. She's no threat to you. Now, please let me go."

Captain Ironskull grinned.

"Thank you sailor, you've been most helpful."

He revved the blade again and swung it towards John's neck.

Daniel stopped reading and closed the book. He had only met those men briefly and hadn't even spoken to most of them but he still felt a terrible sadness when he read about the battle.

"Daniel, are you up? We'll be leaving in five minutes, so if you want some breakfast, come down now."

His mum's voice carried up the stairs the way it always did. Real life came flooding back, with its familiar and safe sounds and smells. Daniel put the book down and went down the stairs, forcing the disturbing words he had read to the back of his mind.

Chapter 5: The Prisoner

Daniel sat next to George at school that afternoon. After talking about football for a while, Daniel mentioned the book.

"Do you remember that old book I had the other day?"

"Yeah."

George was still looking forward, towards the back of the teacher's head as she wrote down a complicated maths problem. Daniel continued, trying to make George interested.

"It's really good. It's about pirates."

"Is it?"

George was still distracted by what the teacher was writing. Daniel lowered his voice, to indicate that what he was saying was secret.

"It's a book you can really get involved with. You can join in and actually go into the story."

George finally turned to face him.

"Like those adventure books, you mean? Turn to page 263 to kill the goblin, that sort of thing?"

Daniel paused as the teacher looked around, fixing them with a glare. Waiting until she was writing again, Daniel replied.

"No, more like…"

He paused. His excitement to share his new world of pirate adventure meant he had said more than he meant to. George was a friend but there was always a chance that he would laugh at Daniel and even worse, tell others and get them to join in the teasing and mockery. It had happened to Daniel all too often in the past. However, seeing George looking interested, he carried on.

"More like actually being there."

George looked puzzled.

"How does that work, with 3D glasses or something? It's an old book, surely they didn't have the technology. Does it just look old?"

Daniel shook his head.

"No, it's not technology. At least, I don't think so. I'm not sure how it works but come round after school and I'll show you."

George raised an eyebrow.

"Don't tell me it's a pop-up book."

Daniel laughed.

"No. Just come round after school and see."

The end of school couldn't come soon enough for Daniel, the final bell ringing out his freedom. As he headed across the playground towards the gate, Barry, Bill and Owen tried to trip him. They started shouting about his mad uncle as he ran off and Daniel hoped that they had better things to do than torment him. Luck was with him; they weren't interested in following as he ran off and they didn't say anything about his book or map. Running past George and out of the gate, Daniel seemed to be keen to get home but really, he was just as keen to avoid contact with the bullies before he got there. George jogged to keep up as he sped off down the road.

"Steady on, it's too hot for all this running."

George was better at sport than Daniel but this afternoon he was right; it was too hot for running. The late spring sun scorched down, drawing sweat from beneath uncomfortable school uniforms and causing itches where school bag straps rubbed on shoulders. Daniel pretended not to hear and ran on to the end of the road, slowing only when he was sure they wouldn't be caught by anyone else. George was keen to stop at the shop and buy a can of drink but Daniel talked him out of it.

"We've probably got lemonade at our house, it won't cost anything. Come on, the sooner we get there the sooner you can have some."

George shrugged and trudged on.

Daniel's mum was out when he arrived home. He and George helped themselves to ginger ale (there was no lemonade) from the kitchen cupboard. Taking the last mouthful of his fizzy liquid, George asked Daniel about the book.

"So, where is it? Are you going to show me how it works or what?"

Daniel felt nervous; what if it did nothing, or even worse, went wrong? After all, he had only made the journey into the world of the pirates once. Starting to regret his rash promise, Daniel took the map out of the case and rolled it out on the table.

"Give me a hair from your head."

"What? Why do you want a hair?"

George looked at him suspiciously.

"Never mind why, just do it. I need it to make the map work."

George shrugged and pulled a hair from the top of his head, making too much of a fuss as he did so. Daniel took it from him and tied it around one of the spare pins. Taking a fresh hair from his own head, he explained the map to George; handing him his pin, Daniel pointed to various parts of the map with his finger.

"These places are ports. Port St David is the biggest, that's where the navy are based. Blackrum is where the pirates live. You have to be careful, and only put your pin into the ports, otherwise you might end up in the middle of the sea, or something."

George seemed to be going along with the idea so far. He looked down at the map as he asked

"Like this, you mean?"

Before Daniel could tell him to stop, George plunged his pin into Port St David. Like a boxer taking a right hook, George collapsed onto the floor, unconscious. Daniel looked down at his sleeping friend.

"George?"

There was no response, even when he shook George vigorously. Feeling panic rise within him, Daniel tied his own hair around his pin and pushed it into Port St David, next to George's.

Daniel came round as before, except this time he was in a tiny cell containing a bunk bed, some dirty straw, some black mould and not a lot else. He was lying on his back on the bottom bunk of the bed. Only one other person was in the room; a smartly dressed naval officer who stood, facing him. It was George. He looked confused.

"Daniel, what's happening? Where are we?"

Daniel shook his head, trying to clear the fuzzy feeling between his ears.

"Just go along with it. Whatever they tell, you, go along with it. They'll call me Tom, I don't know what they'll call you. Just act as if it's all real."

Before George could reply, a second officer appeared at his shoulder.

"Come on. Best not keep The Admiral waiting."

The other officer led them up three flights of stairs without saying a word; George was too shocked to say anything and Daniel soon realised that if George was an officer and they were in Port St David, he was probably a prisoner. He contemplated what this might mean for him as he climbed the spiral staircase. The Admiral, he remembered, hated pirates and now Daniel was a pirate himself. He wondered how he had been captured; the book had not mentioned it so far and he hadn't missed any pages out. A prod between the shoulder blades pulled him back to the staircase. Onwards they climbed, the steps leading ever upwards in semi darkness lit only by occasional slit windows. The windows were too small to see out of so Daniel couldn't use the view to work out where they might be. He guessed it would be a fortress of some sort. He would find out soon enough.

The officer led them to the top of the stairs and into a long room. Sitting in an ornate seat behind a huge desk was the Admiral; standing to his right was Skop Groggen, dressed in the uniform of a naval officer. Daniel stared. Skop Groggen winked, then motioned with his hand towards a much simpler seat in the middle of the room. Daniel sat down, feeling exposed and wondering what was going on. He glanced around; there were no other people in the room. George and the other officer seemed to have vanished although they were probably just waiting behind him. Skop Groggen stood up.

"Please confirm that you are a member of the crew of the notorious pirate, Captain Crimson."

Daniel thought for a few seconds.

"I am, yes."

After a moment, he added

"I'm the cabin boy."

The Admiral leaned forward. He jabbed his finger towards Daniel as he spoke.

"See, the boy is condemned by his own mouth. He consorts with pirates and has confessed it; he shall be subject to the full force of the law."

Skop Groggen whispered something in the Admiral's ear. He nodded and sat back into his seat.

"However, on this occasion we may be persuaded to show clemency, if his testimony proves useful to us. We are not without mercy for those who cooperate with the process of justice and who turn from their wicked ways. Continue with the questioning, Mr. Church."

Skop Groggen touched his temple in a salute.

"Of course sir."

Skop Groggen, or Mr Church, turned to face Daniel once more.

"Now, lad. Is it true that Captain Crimson has sent you to talk to the Royal Navy? Has she sent you to negotiate an alliance between the Navy and selected pirates?"

Daniel paused. He had no idea what the right answer was but Skop Groggen nodded once. Daniel answered.

"That's true."

The Admiral frowned.

"So, the pirates seek our aid? Why is this?"

Skop Groggen spoke before Daniel had to.

"I believe the pirates see an opportunity which may help both us and them."

The Admiral's frown deepened.

"And why has she sent her cabin boy to perform the negotiations? Why does the rapscallion not come herself?"

The real answer, Daniel thought, was that the cabin boy was the least valuable member of the crew. If the Admiral decided to hang him, it would cause least problems to Captain Crimson, who was already short of men. Yet once again, before he had to think of something to tell the Admiral, Skop Groggen spoke up.

"It is a sign of good faith, sir. She places the most vulnerable member of her crew in your hands, the one who is least able to resist should you decide to take him prisoner or subject him to naval justice. She is showing that it is the Navy which has the power in this situation. She is throwing herself on your mercy, sir."

Daniel considered that it wasn't Captain Crimson who was thrown on the Admiral's mercy at all, it was him. However, the reply seemed to please the Admiral, who changed the subject.

"So, what is this opportunity that the female rogue sees? What does she require of us that leads her to jeopardise a member of her crew?"

Daniel paused once more, hoping that Skop Groggen (or Mr Church) would speak for him. He glanced up but only saw the penetrating eyes of the Admiral, drilling a hole into him. He managed to find some courage to speak.

"She wishes to make a deal with you."

The Admiral's eyes remained fixed.

"What sort of deal would this rogue want from us?"

Daniel waited again, but it was left for him to fill the silence. He wondered what Skop Groggen was playing at; Why wasn't he helping anymore? He tried to think of something else to say, to stall for time.

"One which will help us both."

The silence seemed to last for ages. Daniel continued.

"That is, one which will help both the navy and the pirates."

Now Skop Groggen chose to speak.

"I believe the boy is speaking of the Pirate Ironskull. You know that he attacks his own kind?"

The Admiral nodded once, glancing across at Skop Groggen.

"I have been informed that he has been attacking pirates as well as honest traders and has even gone so far as to challenge our good warships."

Daniel felt brave, so he spoke again, almost shouting over the Admiral.

"That's what I came to say. We should join forces against him!"

The Admiral turned his gaze back on Daniel; Daniel wished he hadn't. The Admiral spoke slowly, as if talking to someone who couldn't speak his language.

"Better men than you, boy, have been flogged to within an inch of their lives for interrupting me. You are a pirate and would have been hanged already were it not for my supreme mercy, which grows thin when I am angered by the insolence of boys who should know their place and speak only when questioned. I suggest you remember this, speak when given leave to do so and do not interrupt your betters again."

Skop Groggen cleared his throat.

"With every respect due to your elevated position, sir, this is the offer that the boy has been sent to give. The lady pirate wishes to assist the navy in capturing or sinking the pirate Ironskull."

The Admiral smiled. It was the smile of a cat which has its paw on the neck of a mouse.

"What is to prevent us attacking and sinking this Ironskull ourselves? Why should we call on the aid of a disorganised rabble?"

Daniel had no idea what to say to that. He was scared to speak and equally scared not to. He tried making something up on the spot.

"We, that is Captain Crimson and the crew of the Crimson Firedrake, know where to find him and how to defeat him. You need our help."

Skop Groggen took over, much to Daniel's relief.

"Indeed, sir. The lady pirate does indeed have knowledge which may be of use. If I might take a few ships and make the arrangements to sail…"

The Admiral cut him off with a wave of his arm.

"Mr Church, I have not yet consented to this agreement. As you know, my aim is to rid these waters of the menace of piracy; making bargains with the very reprobates I seek to eliminate strikes me as a poor way to achieve this. Tell me why I should not just have this boy clapped in irons and used as a warning to others of his kind?"

Skop Groggen spoke; for the first time, his words were slow, as if he was thinking as he spoke. His sudden lack of confidence worried Daniel.

"Well, sir, there is more than one way to end the menace of the pirates. If you were to offer this lady a full pardon on condition that she gave up her life of crime, I'm sure she would prove most helpful, and ultimately we would have two fewer pirates to worry about."

The Admiral sat in silence, torn between his need to remove the greater threat and his desire to see all pirates brought to justice. Long seconds passed. Eventually, he pronounced his judgement. Daniel waited, nerves on edge, to hear what he said.

"Any such pardon would only come into effect on the full elimination of the pirate Ironskull and on my own personal agreement that the female pirate has performed all we ask. We will require some form of guarantee that she will not attempt anything foolish once she has fulfilled her part of any plan and a further guarantee that she will not return to a life of piracy. As such, you will be my personal representative on that pirate's ship Mr Church, along with as many armed fighting men as you need. I will also require that a senior crew member from her ship is kept aboard the naval flagship throughout the operation. Someone of greater significance than this boy."

Skop Groggen grinned.

"Of course sir. Shall I command this operation from the pirate vessel?"

The Admiral stood, raising his shoulders and drawing himself up to his full height.

"No. This excursion shall be led by me personally Mr Church. Now, you may all dismiss and make preparations to set sail. We leave at dawn."

With that, the Admiral turned and strode out of the room. Skop Groggen waited for the Admiral to close the door behind him, then crossed the floor to Daniel. He called to the two officers, George and the other man.

"Gentlemen, set about making the necessary arrangements."

The other officer clicked his heels together, saluted smartly and left the room. George remained where he was, looking uncertain. Daniel summoned him over with a flick of his hand.

"This is my friend George, from the other place."

Skop Groggen raised an eyebrow. Daniel carried on talking.

"So, what on earth is going on? Why am I here as a prisoner and why are you one of the Admiral's top men?"

Skop Groggen looked a little shame faced.

"It was the plan, Tom. I know it seems unfair that you had to be handed over for a night in the dungeon while I get to enjoy the Admiral's company."

Daniel couldn't tell if Skop Groggen was being sarcastic. He didn't have time to ask as the old man carried on with his explanation.

"Anyway, as you know, we had to convince the Admiral to let us take his fleet. A plan that was mostly successful."

"Mostly?"

Skop Groggen sighed.

"It was part of the plan that the Admiral would let me command the fleet. He hasn't sailed in about ten years, how was I to know he'd want to command the fleet himself?"

Daniel looked across at his friend. George was still standing, open mouthed, trying to take it all in. This, he thought, would take some explaining. He turned back to Skop Groggen.

"Why is that important?"

Skop Groggen glanced towards the door.

"Because we wanted the navy ships and firepower to be under our command. Now we'll have to deal with the Admiral himself, and he will insist on leading the whole operation. Our plans will have to change."

Daniel's question was framed with a single word.

"Why?"

Skop Groggen put an arm around his shoulder and steered him away, obviously not trusting George the officer despite Daniel's claim.

"Because our plan involves doing things that the Admiral might not agree with. Now, it's all going to be far more difficult. Now come on, we must get going."

George, who had been walking a few steps behind them, almost bumped into them as they turned.

"Get going? Where?"

Skop Groggen replied, in an authoritative tone.

"Did you not hear the Admiral, officer? We sail at dawn. We are going to meet with the pirates."

Chapter 6: Captain Firebeard and the Council of War

George was already sitting on the bed when Daniel came round.

"What on earth happened there?"

George looked stunned. Daniel had been separated from him after they had been taken to the ships; as before, he had fallen asleep in a hammock and woken in his room. George didn't appear to have been awake for long but Daniel asked him anyway.

"When did you wake up?"

George rubbed his eyes, trying to clear his head.

"Just now. I was taken to the officer's quarters and I sat down for a moment in an old armchair. I think I fell asleep and I've woken up back here."

He paused for a few seconds, trying to think of the words to say. His mouth flapped like a landed fish; in the end, he managed to collect his thoughts enough to ask

"Daniel, what happened?"

Daniel shrugged, trying to look casual.

"We went into the book world."

This prompted more fish mouthed flapping before George responded,

"How?"

George looked worried and confused in equal measure. Daniel replied with some hesitation.

"I'm not sure exactly how it works. Something to do with the map and the book."

The explanation sounded weak even to Daniel. George looked at his watch.

"We've been asleep for an hour. It seemed like longer while we were there."

This was a surprise to Daniel.

"Really? Last time I was there, I woke up the next day."

George stood up, holding onto the side of a chair.

"Does the book say anything about what just happened?"

Daniel nodded.

"It will be written down there. If we read on, other things will happen and we won't be able to go in and change them."

George walked to the door.

"I don't think I want to go back and change them. It's all a bit too weird for me. I'm off home. See you later, Daniel."

Daniel saw George out. George was clearly shaken by what had happened, although he tried to maintain his usual aura of cool. As his friend disappeared down the road, Daniel dashed upstairs and started to read the next chapter of the book.

Blackrum was deserted. Every pirate ship and pirate captain had left for open water as soon as they saw the naval fleet approaching; all except Captain Crimson and Captain Firebeard, who had been told about the coming fleet and invited to meet with the naval officers. Now, only a handful of people sat inside the Inn of the She Wolf and that meeting was nothing like the usual gatherings which took place there. This meeting was formal and while there was wine and ale available, nobody was even a little bit drunk. The landlord of the inn, keen to make whatever money he could, had given them his best room for the meeting. It was large and had a high ceiling but it was not good enough for the Admiral, who sat at the head of the table and complained.

"I would have hoped that the proprietor of this establishment would see fit to clean this room to appropriate standards for an officer of my elevated standing. As it is, I doubt that this place has seen the presence of a broom since it was first thrown together from whatever flotsam and debris have been used in the construction of this poor excuse for a tavern. It may be acceptable for a gathering of drunken reprobates who care not what foul diseases and ravenous insects lurk in every filthy crevice but I expect significantly better for a naval conference, gentlemen."

This had set the tone for the meeting. As the Admiral fussed with his seat and complained to his officers, the pirate captains entered with their most important crew members and took up their seats at the table. Captain Firebeard and Captain Crimson disliked one another intensely, and their rivalry came out as soon as they sat down at the table. They sat opposite one another and stared, like cats lining up for a fight. Captain Firebeard, not recognising Skop Groggen in his naval uniform, started the taunting.

"So, Captain Crimson, it appears that you have lost your Wizard. Did he finally remember that it's terrible bad luck to sail with a woman? Or did he get tired of ambushing fishing boats for copper scraps and fish heads?"

Captain Crimson smiled, and stabbed a jewel handled dagger into the table top.

"Copper scraps and fish heads? My, how entertaining you are, Captain Firebeard. You should ask if the King needs a court jester. As far as treasure goes, I would ask you which of us has recently come into several hundred gold coins,"

She glanced across at the naval officers at the end of the table, nodding at them as she carried on, "through legitimate trading, of course, and which of us has nothing but fish in his hold. Rotten fish, at that."

Captain Firebeard stood up. His booming voice filled the room as his finger jabbed towards his rival.

"You know something of that, do you? Only the most childish of sailors would put rotten fish in a more successful captain's hold. Is that why your wizard left? He got fed up with your childish antics?"

Captain Crimson remained seated, although she picked up her dagger.

"If I had the choice of no wizard or your wizard, I think I'd stick with none. By taking that man to sea, you are depriving a village of its idiot."

She pointed towards Captain Firebeard's wizard, a spindly old man who was already asleep in the corner. Captain Firebeard opened his mouth to reply but the Admiral cut him off.

"I have no wish to listen to the arguing of criminals and ne'er-do-wells. I wish to conclude this meeting as rapidly as possible and return to places which are fit for civilised humans to inhabit."

The bickering pirates turned to face the Admiral, who carried on.

"I have come to this wretched pit of debauchery on the advice of a most able officer. He will now explain to you our purpose; Mr Church, please explain as simply as you are able to this assembly of rogues and rapscallions what it is we seek from them."

Skop Groggen rose from his seat next to the Admiral. Recognition dawned on the face of Captain Firebeard, but despite his surprise, he remained silent. Skop Groggen performed a small bow towards the Admiral, then began to speak.

"We have come because we have a common enemy; an enemy whose power has grown in recent times and who commands strange energies and dangerous machinery. I speak of the pirate, Captain Ironskull; his influence has become such a significant threat that we are now willing to do what would normally be unthinkable; we are prepared to make an alliance with you, the most important among the pirate captains, in order to deal with him."

Captain Firebeard interrupted.

"So, Mr Church. What is it you want from us, and how do we know we can trust you? The navy has hanged every man accused of piracy, innocent or guilty, that has been captured in these waters. How do we know you won't hang us as soon as Captain Ironskull is out of the way?"

The Admiral turned purple with rage.

"You dare to accuse me of dishonesty?"

Skop Groggen carried on talking, covering over the Admiral's anger with his answer.

"The navy would ask something similar in return; how can we trust that you will not abandon the alliance at the first opportunity, and return to a life of crime? The answer for both sides is as follows; we will provide you with letters which amount to a full pardon for any crimes of piracy committed before the alliance; furthermore, the letters will provide you with a salary each year in the future, in return for your work on behalf of the navy. However, during our alliance, we will insist that an officer of the navy is present on board each ship, and that one of your most important crew members is sent aboard the naval flagship, HMS Cantankerous, until Captain Ironskull is defeated. Agree to these terms and there will be no need for any hangings."

Captain Firebeard nodded slowly, drips of ale falling from his huge beard.

"That seems fair enough."

He thought for a few seconds more, his head nodding back and forth like a boulder on a clifftop. Then a calculating grin appeared behind the mass of red hair around his mouth.

"If I agree, I want you to be the naval officer aboard my ship. You seem like the sort of man I could trust. I'm very particular about the type of officer I allow onto my ship."

Captain Crimson raised an eyebrow.

"You seem very quick to accept the deal, Captain Firebeard. Do you know something that the rest of us don't? Have you been talking with these officers in advance, perhaps?"

Skop Groggen shook his head before Captain Firebeard could answer.

"Indeed not, lady. As for which officer is assigned to which ship, that decision must rest with the Admiral. Part of the agreement is that he must be in command of the alliance. While each of you will have control over your ships and will be involved in the planning, this will be a naval operation. As such, I am sure he will wish to consult with his officers before we set sail, to decide who will go where."

Captain Firebeard looked towards the Admiral.

"Mr Admiral, sir. Can I have this man as the representative on board my ship? If so, I agree to the deal."

The Admiral and Skop Groggen both looked shocked by this sudden development. The Admiral spoke first.

"Well, if that is your only requirement then you can consider it agreed. Mr Church, you will serve aboard Captain Firebeard's ship for the duration of this alliance, as the representative of the navy. Now hand the letters of agreement to Captain Firebeard, if you please."

Skop Groggen, still shocked, handed over the letters. Captain Firebeard looked at them.

"These scribbles are all very pretty but I'll need to get them looked at by someone who understands such things. My wizard is a man of letters. He will check them for me."

He stood, turned and kicked the stool out from under his wizard. The old man fell onto the floor in a spluttering tangle of arms and legs.

"Wizard! I need you to look at these papers!"

The old man unfolded himself from the floor. He held the papers too close to his nose.

"They say you have to work for the navy so they don't hang you. They say you get let off for being a pirate once Ironskull is beaten and they say you get paid fifty gold pieces every year. You have to write your name at the bottom."

Captain Firebeard waved towards the old man.

"Wizard, you can write my name. That's your job."

The Admiral shook his head.

"No, it must be you that signs your name."

Captain Firebeard sat down uncomfortably. He took the papers and looked at them. Skop Groggen leaned forward.

"Can you write, Captain Firebeard?"

Captain Firebeard looked miserable.

"I have the wizard to write when things need writing. I'm good at swinging a war axe and sailing a ship. I have no need for writing."

The Admiral snapped in irritation.

"Well, if you cannot write, simply put a cross."

Captain Firebeard scowled.

"Which way up should the cross be?"

The Admiral lost the little bit of patience he had left.

"I don't care if you draw a little face with a beard! As long as you make your mark and agree to the alliance, the document is legal!"

Captain Firebeard took the paper and the quill with a flourish. He drew a little picture of a man with a big beard, carrying an axe. When he finished, he handed the letter to Skop Groggen, holding it as if it was a holy artefact. Skop Groggen took it, looked at it, showed it to the Admiral who nodded, then handed it back.

"You keep this, Captain Firebeard. It is your proof that you are no longer a wanted pirate."

Captain Firebeard handed the letter to his wizard. Skop Groggen looked towards Captain Crimson.

"Do you also intend to join the alliance?"

Captain Crimson took the papers.

"I'm still not clear exactly what our role will be. Surely the navy has the firepower to defeat Captain Ironskull and if not, I don't see what adding two pirate ships will do apart from get us all sunk together."

She had spoken to Skop Groggen, clearly waiting for a planned reply. However the Admiral replied before Skop Groggen had the chance.

"Believe me, it gives me no pleasure at all to have to deal with pirates and if there was any alternative course open, I would take it. However, our warships have had little luck in finding this Captain Ironskull and have reason to believe you can lead us to him. We need him defeated with all haste; we cannot have him loose in these waters. This, along with your knowledge of how the pirate will think is enough to make us offer this alliance. Be aware that we will only offer it once."

Captain Crimson took the papers. She glanced at them for a moment before giving her reply.

"I am going to want a little more than Captain Firebeard before I agree to sign."

The Admiral regarded her down the length of his nose.

"State your terms."

Captain Crimson paused for effect before she replied.

"I want to keep any treasure I manage to obtain in destroying Captain Ironskull; your letter doesn't mention treasure and I know you naval types like to seize all you can for the crown. I want to retain full command of the Crimson Firedrake throughout any engagements; your officer is a member of my crew and does as he is commanded while on board. I want the right to disagree with any plan and the right to opt out if I don't agree with it. There are my terms."

She offered her hand to the Admiral. He regarded it.

"I cannot agree to the last point. Once you are in the alliance, you must do as commanded. I can give you the right to have a one third vote on any plan but once a plan is agreed, it must have the full commitment of the alliance."

Captain Crimson looked at Skop Groggen; nobody but them noticed him nod once. Captain Crimson offered her hand again.

"If you agree that we each have a one third vote, I accept these terms."

The Admiral ignored the hand.

"Sign the papers if you please, Captain Crimson."

Captain Crimson signed in flowing handwriting.

"Now, Admiral. Shall we get down to planning, or shall we have a drink first?"

Everyone except the Admiral wanted to pause for a drink. The Admiral was annoyed by this but was convinced to allow it by Skop Groggen, especially as Captain Firebeard was persuaded to pay. Once all of the drinks were poured, the meeting turned to the matter of how to find Captain Ironskull. The Admiral turned first to Captain Crimson.

"Now, lady. Your role within this alliance is to help us find Captain Ironskull. How do you plan to do this?"

Captain Crimson leaned forward. Everyone else leaned forward too, as her eyes darted from one to the other.

"It is a great and terrible secret of the pirates, that I am about to tell you."

Even the Admiral was captivated; he also leaned forward as Captain Crimson spoke in little more than a whisper.

"We shall journey to the Island of Thunder, where the dead are said to walk. There, if we are able to pass by the Dead Guardians, we shall consult with the Oracle of the Deep, whose wisdom extends to the depths of the ocean. From him, we shall learn how to defeat our foe, though the cost may be terrible."

While she spoke, the lamps flickered and dimmed. A chill was felt through the room and nervous pirate eyes glanced towards dark corners, in case something evil should happen to them for even speaking the name of the Oracle of the Deep. Then the Admiral snorted and all returned to normal.

"What absolute and complete nonsense! You tell us fairy tales when we should be planning a military operation, Captain Crimson! There is no such island, for one thing…"

Captain Crimson kept her cool.

"The island's location is a secret known only to the sea wizards. All others could search for ever and a day but would sail right past without ever knowing it was there. It will not be marked on your charts, Admiral."

The Admiral couldn't hide his annoyance.

"Have you no suggestions suitable for our purpose? I would remind you that our alliance and your pardon are based on finding Captain Ironskull, not entertaining us with your superstitious bedtime stories."

Many of the naval officers joined in with the Admiral. Captain Firebeard agreed, more to annoy Captain Crimson than because he actually thought that the Admiral was right. The mood in the room turned sour; Captain Crimson suggested that they should use Captain Firebeard as bait to catch Captain Ironskull, as his large belly would be easiest to spot for the iron pirate. Captain Crimson then went on to suggest that perhaps Captain Firebeard had employed a wizard who had no idea how to find the Oracle of the Seas which was the reason for his arguing. Captain Firebeard's wizard denied this, saying that he was quite capable of finding his way to the Oracle. Captain Crimson continued with her attack on the wizard.

"You couldn't find your way to the latrines if you had an extra nose, let alone find your way to the Oracle of the Seas."

Captain Crimson leant her chair back on two legs as she mocked him. The Admiral tried to interrupt once more, expressing his view that there was no such thing as the Oracle of *the Seas. However the wizard, in a rare moment of emotion, shouted back at Captain Crimson, overpowering even the Admiral's words.*

"Not only can I find the Oracle, I have been there within the past few weeks and spoken with him, face to face! I could lead you straight to him now!"

Captain Crimson grinned, crossing her legs as her feet rested on the table.

"So, do you still think it nonsense that there is an Oracle of the Seas, Captain Firebeard? Your wizard claims to have visited him. Surely that proves the matter, unless you want to call your own wizard a liar."

Captain Firebeard was lost for words. On the one hand, he had already agreed with the Admiral that the Oracle was just a myth; on the other hand, to hold to that view would be to undermine his wizard in public. He was stuck and he knew it. Captain Crimson pressed her point.

"If your wizard knows the way, let him lead us there. If he is wrong, then clearly the Admiral's opinion, which you have already agreed with, is correct and we will need another plan. However, if your wizard speaks the truth, then not only can he find the Oracle, he has already passed the Dead Guardians and spoken with him. If he has done it once, he could do it again."

The Admiral remained silent. He looked towards Skop Groggen who slapped his palm on the table three times.

"We must vote on this proposal. How do you declare, Captain Firebeard?"

Captain Firebeard tried to save face with his reply.

"I vote that we follow my wizard's plan. He knows more of these matters than any of us."

Skop Groggen's raised eyebrow went unnoticed as Captain Crimson joined in.

"Well said, Captain! I agree, which makes two of us. Under the agreement, that is a two-thirds majority Admiral. The plan is agreed."

The Admiral stood, ready to leave the room.

"As much as I hate to say it, I am bound to the plan, foolish as it sounds. However, if this turns out to be a waste of time, I will hold you all to account for it. Mr Church, prepare our ships for departure. We sail on the next tide."

Chapter 7: Owen and the Ambush

George was noticeably distant with Daniel the next day at school. He refused to speak about what had happened, although he did agree to go back to Daniel's house after school when Daniel suggested that they should play computer games, and didn't mention the book. Daniel's mum was already at home when they arrived. She was tidying the kitchen and greeted them with a distracted smile.

"Go and play in the living room, there's good boys. I've got to tidy up, there's a visitor coming."

Daniel and George hadn't even managed to turn the computer on when there was a knock at the door.

"Will you get that please, Daniel? I'm up to my elbows in washing up."

Daniel scrambled towards the door, knocking aside cushions and schoolbags as he went. He got a shock when he opened the door; standing next to a tall blonde woman was Owen. Owen was equally surprised to see him, a surprise which was written all over his face. Daniel paused for a moment, speechless before his mum's voice, shouting from the kitchen, pulled him back to reality.

"Daniel, aren't you going to invite our guests in?"

Daniel tried not to stammer and failed.

"Erm… come in… I… Pleased to meet… I'm Daniel."

The woman looked down towards him, not unkindly but in the way that one might regard a toddler that had knocked over the milk.

"Yes. I'm Mrs McCormack. I'm here to see your mother. Shall we come in?"

Daniel gestured towards the kitchen.

"Please, be my guest."

He tried not to flinch as Owen walked past but the bully made no move towards him; he didn't even look at Daniel as he followed his mother into the kitchen.

"You boys can go and play while we talk about our display."

Daniel groaned inwardly. The local artists group was holding a display and Daniel's mum was involved in organising it. Owen's mum was also involved, so while they discussed art displays in the kitchen, the boys were expected to go and play somewhere else. Daniel had never mentioned that

Owen was involved in making his life miserable at school and he was certain that Owen wouldn't have mentioned it to his mum either, so they were sent off together while their mothers drank tea and planned their display.

"You'd better come this way."

Daniel tried not to appear frightened. At least George was still there.

"Haven't you got any good games?"

Owen had returned to his usual personality once their mothers were out of earshot. George had greeted Owen's arrival with a relaxed nod; easy for him, Daniel thought, as he's not the one who has to suffer Owen's attentions at school. George had explained that they were about to play some computer games; Owen had looked at the games on offer and sneered. Owen liked computer games but none of the games Daniel owned were violent enough for him; none featured zombies or chainsaws, which seemed to be his favourite combination. Daniel had suggested a war game, but Owen had rejected it due to the lack of graphic on-screen killing. Daniel started to get annoyed.

"Why don't you go and get some of your games, then? We'll wait here, we can play them when you get back."

For a moment, Daniel thought that his plan might work. Owen looked tempted by the suggestion. The hope popped like a bubble a second later.

"I think I'll stay here. If you can't find me something decent to play, I might just play wrestling, against you. For real."

George, who had been sitting in silence, spoke up.

"Why don't you show Owen your book, Daniel?"

Daniel felt the cold claw of dread in his stomach. He tried to catch George's eye, to let him know that he shouldn't mention the book or the map to Owen but it was too late.

"Is this the book that your mad uncle gave you?"

Daniel tried to change the subject.

"It's just an old book, it's very boring. You'd hate it. We could go outside and play football."

George, failing to see what Daniel was trying to do, carried on talking about the book.

"It's not boring, it's amazing. I don't know how it works, but…"

Daniel cut him off, trying to shut down the idea before it started.

"If you really want to see it, I'll show you. You won't be very excited though, it's just an old book."

It failed. With a sneer, Owen agreed to look at the book.

Daniel hoped to grab a word with George on the way upstairs, to warn him to keep quiet about the book and the map. It didn't happen. Owen forced his way between Daniel and George, making rude remarks all the way up to Daniel's bedroom. Once there, he caught sight of the map and the pins. He pointed at the remains of the footprint which were still visible on the corner of the map.

"Looks like someone's trodden on your map, Danny boy."

George, still failing to pick up on the tension in the room, pointed at the pins.

"Show him what those can do, Daniel."

Owen picked up a pin.

"I know what these can do. Shall I stick one in your leg and see how far you jump?"

George picked up the pin with his hair tied around it.

"I don't know how it works, but it seems to be a sort of DNA based virtual reality thing. Daniel, show Owen how it works."

Daniel hoped that he could put Owen off and shut George up with his response.

"Ok. Owen, I need you to pull a hair out of your head and give it to me. Then I'll stick it into the map and it'll take you off to pirate world. It's a game I was playing with George the other day."

Daniel knew that this would lead to mockery from Owen but that would be coming anyway; by bringing George into it, he might be able to shut him up. However, George jumped in before Owen could speak.

"It really does take you into the pirate world. I don't know how the game works, but it's amazing. Go on Owen, you won't believe it."

Owen looked at George with suspicion.

"Are you trying to have a laugh at me? If you are, I'll smack you so hard…"

George interrupted again.

"I'm not, honestly. Daniel, tell him."

Daniel shrugged.

"Like I say, it's a game we were playing. Join in if you want."

Owen looked at them both. Daniel expected a rude remark or threat. He was shocked when Owen reached up and plucked a hair from his head. He held it out towards Daniel.

"Go on then. Show me what your mad uncle's book can do. Impress me."

Daniel knew that Owen wanted an excuse to bully him more. He tied the hair around the pin; for a second, he was tempted to stick it into a remote island but instead, he jabbed it into Blackrum Port. Owen slumped to the floor, banging his head on the table as he went down. Daniel felt a moment of guilty pleasure at that.

"What do we do now?"

George looked at Daniel, waiting for him to take the lead. Daniel shrugged.

"Follow him, I suppose."

Daniel came round on board ship. The groggy head and confusion faded more quickly this time; Daniel supposed that he must be getting used to it. Looking around, he saw that the ship was about to set sail. Standing on the deck a few paces away, looking stunned, was Owen. Daniel walked over to him, trying not to grin.

"Welcome aboard the Crimson Firedrake. It looks like we're about to leave so you'd better get ready to do some work."

Owen stared at him.

"How is this happening?"

Daniel shrugged.

"Don't know. I just know that it is. You'd better go along with it."

Owen reached for a belaying pin lying on the deck nearby.

"Make it stop, or I'll bash your head in with this."

Daniel took a step back.

"I can't. It stops when it stops. You'd better start working or there'll be trouble."

Boulder had noticed the two of them talking to each other. He strode over, slapping Owen around the back of the head as he frowned at them.

"You need to get to your places and get ready to make sail. The Captain wants us to be the best crew, remember? That won't happen if you stand about doing nothing."

Owen dodged a further blow as he was led away. Daniel found it hard to feel sympathy for him.

They left the harbour under full sail; the unusual sight of pirate ships leading naval ships out to open water would have been met with some surprise had there been anyone left in Blackrum Port to see it. Captain Firebeard had edged his ship ahead and as the harbour mouth was narrow, Captain Crimson had to give way and wait as her rival sailed through the gap. Boulder blamed this on Owen, who avoided a severe beating only due to the amount of work that had to be done; Boulder was too busy to batter him there and then, but promised that as soon as they were on the ocean he would have "the thrashing of his life." Captain Firebeard waved as he sailed by, obviously enjoying the moment. Daniel stared; the naval officer standing next to him on the poop deck was George. Daniel waved but George either didn't dare return the wave or didn't see him. Captain Crimson kicked a coil of rope in annoyance.

"As if it wasn't bad enough having to put my wizard on his ship. Now he's going to get to the Oracle before we do and claim all of the credit for leading the Admiral there. I hate that man."

Daniel thought it was better not to point out that without Skop Groggen, Captain Crimson wouldn't find the Oracle anyway. As Captain Firebeard's ship pulled away, Captain Crimson's crew began turning their ship to navigate the narrow passage. Again, Owen became the target of Boulder's anger. Having never set foot on a sailing ship before, Owen didn't know what to do and several times his efforts worked against the rest of the crew. Eventually, Boulder sent him away with a boot up the backside, telling him to throw himself overboard to make the ship lighter if he could be no use any other way. Daniel felt a twinge of pity until Owen gave him a dead arm as he passed.

"You've set this up just to torment me. I'll make you pay once it's over."

By the time they cleared the harbour mouth, Captain Firebeard's sails were shrinking squares against the horizon. Daniel could hear the Admiral shouting from HMS Cantankerous behind them. He couldn't hear the words but he knew that the Admiral was angry and that the anger was probably directed towards Captain Crimson. He walked away from the stern rail; Owen was doing something on the port side of the ship so Daniel kept to Starboard as he approached the bow. Captain Crimson was standing there, holding her hat in her hand so that the wind didn't whip it away. Her hair blew crazily around her face. Daniel stood next to her.

"Can we catch them up?"

Captain Crimson kept looking forward.

"Possibly, if his crew are lazy or stupid, which they are. We'll have to be at our best if we want to catch them, though. They've nearly reached Grey Island and it's plain sailing from there."

Daniel looked behind him.

"What about the Admiral?"

Captain Crimson snorted.

"He's a pompous old blowhard. As long as I'm on my ship and he's on his, he can do what he likes. The less time I have to spend around him, the better, which is another reason not to hang about."

Daniel looked forward across the water. The dark mass of Grey Island could now be seen next to Captain Firebeard's sails, looming like a hulk against the cloudy sky.

"Something's not right."

Captain Crimson was squinting forward, using her hat to shield her eyes. Daniel looked across the water. The ship ahead was turning; it was moving around, to sail towards the island. Daniel was about to ask his captain what they were doing when he saw several flashes of light reflected across the rocks and the water, like a thunderstorm on the horizon.

"That's cannon fire! They're under attack!"

The boom of the cannons reached them a second or two later. Captain Crimson jumped up onto the rail and started shouting instructions to the crew.

"Full speed! I want every sail bent to bursting; blow into them yourselves if you have to! Run out the cannons and arm yourselves! We have a fight to join!"

Daniel watched as a sinister shape emerged from behind the island. Long, like a ship but with chimney pipes instead of sails, it slid across the water towards its prey like a metal shark. Captain Firebeard was trying to turn his ship to bring his cannons to bear but the attacker was already firing; Daniel could see a turret on the bow, the cannon flashing as it fired on the pirates. He realised what was happening and yelled above the general hubbub;

"It's Captain Ironskull!"

Captain Crimson stared forwards again and swore. Captain Firebeard was firing back but his shots were doing no obvious damage to the metal ship. The gap to the battle was closing; Daniel glanced backwards, and saw that the naval warships were behind them; they had also seen the battle and were racing to help.

"Why didn't we see them?"

Daniels question drew a frustrated shrug from Captain Crimson.

"I don't know. They might've been waiting on the far side of the island."

Daniel realised that was unlikely, unless Captain Ironskull had known when they were leaving and where they planned to go. Surely that was impossible? Another blast from the turret took down one of Captain Firebeard's masts; Daniel was now close enough to see the men falling from the rigging into the sea.

"Stand ready boys, we'll be in fighting range in two minutes."

Boulder had taken command of the deck party and was handing out muskets. Daniel saw Owen take a musket and step towards the rail, testing the weapon for weight and aim as he did so. The sounds of the battle were getting louder now, screams, yells and gunfire could be heard alongside the booming of the cannons. More and more pieces of Captain Firebeard's ship flew apart under the hail of cannon fire; a second mast fell, slamming onto the deck with a horrifying crash. The ship was starting to list badly. A voice next to Daniel spoke in little more than a whisper.

"If we'd beaten them out of the harbour, that could've been us."

Daniel realised that this was true. He looked at who had spoken; it was Mr Higgs, the bosun. Daniel replied, trying to keep the fear from his voice.

"It could be us in a minute."

Captain Crimson turned the ship as they approached; the bosun explained to Daniel that his was to get the cannons in range.

"She's going to want to fire a full broadside at that iron ship. We just have to hope we can hit hard enough to sink her, or at least do her some damage. Nobody else has even managed that so far, so I'm told."

Daniel could see the pirates on the deck of the iron ship; all had mechanical parts. He wondered whether these had replaced bits they had lost in battle. Among them stood Captain Ironskull, at least a foot taller than anyone else on the deck and more machine than pirate. Soon Daniel's attention was drawn to Captain Crimson's skill, or the skill of her helmsman. They had sailed around to the back of the iron ship while keeping out of the firing line of its cannons. Now their own cannons were in a position to blast their enemy at close range.

It was at that moment that Daniel noticed the turret, rising from the stern. The great cannon it held turned towards them like an accusing finger.

"Watch for the turret!" Daniel's call was in vain; the monstrous weapon spat towards them, smashing into the bow and sending splinters of wood flying in all directions. As if woken from sleep, their own cannons fired, smoke rising in great clouds from the side of the ship, hiding the enemy from view. As it cleared, Daniel could see two things; first, that Captain Firebeard's ship was sinking and second, that their cannons had done very little damage to Captain Ironskull's vessel, just a few dents. A few of Captain Ironskull's crew had been blasted into pieces or knocked into the water but the rest of them didn't seem to care. The turret turned again, preparing to deliver another blast of fire and death. Captain Crimson swore, and ran to the rail. Her shout was towards her enemy rather than her own crew.

"Captain Ironskull! This battle is between captains, not pirate crews! Meet me in single combat, and we will end this!"

A voice replied, as if broadcast through an amplifier. Daniel could see him on the deck, ignoring the shots and splinters that flew all around him.

"Why? You have your friends from the navy coming. If I stay to fight you, they will join in the battle and my ship might be dented."

The metallic crewmen laughed. Captain Ironskull pointed towards Captain Crimson with a blade attached to the end of his mechanical arm.

"One day I will face you one on one, Crimson, but not today. You go and tell the other pirates what I have done to Firebeard. Tell them it's what I do to all my enemies. I'll deal with you when I choose to and not before. Live in fear, Crimson! Your time will come!"

With that, Captain Ironskull powered his ship away, ramming through the burning wreck of Captain Firebeard's vessel. It fell in half, the last few men aboard jumping into the water. All of the surviving crew were now in the water; some were swimming towards the approaching navy while others were being dragged out of the water by Captain Ironskull's machine men. Daniel watched, helpless, as Captain Ironskull sailed further away; Captain Crimson was bringing the Firedrake about but it wasn't fast enough. More men were dragged out of the water onto the iron ship and now Daniel noticed that they were being cut down by the swords and axes of the half-mechanical pirates.

"They're killing them!"

Captain Crimson swore again.

"We'll never get there in time to save them. There's nothing we can do."

The turret fired again, a parting shot and this time it missed them. However, Daniel was more worried about something going on behind it. Near the stern, underneath the turret, a young naval officer was being dragged from the water. Daniel saw immediately that it was George. He watched in horror as a mechanical arm holding a sword was lifted above him. Daniel didn't want to watch but couldn't look away. Then he saw Captain Ironskull himself step forward and stop the blow. As Daniel looked on, powerless to help, Captain Ironskull lifted George up to his eye level. He said a few words to the young officer, who nodded frantically as his feet dangled in the air. Then, with a twist of his arm, Captain Ironskull threw George into the sea.

"Man overboard! Put about, we need to pick him up!"

Daniel's shout was met with a glance of contempt by Mr Higgs.

"There's more important things to do boy. We've got to catch Captain Ironskull and send him to the deep."

It was too late though, and they knew it. Captain Ironskull was already escaping, powering through the water towards the island. Those who weren't helping desperate sailors out of the water could only watch as the iron ship pulled away, vanishing around the island once again. However they were all surprised when it failed to appear on the far side. Boulder stared with wide eyes.

"They've vanished!"

Mr Higgs spat overboard.

"It's not natural. He's in league with evil powers, I tell you."

Captain Crimson stared, not believing her eyes. She was about to speak when a slimy hand appeared over the bow rail, covered in seaweed. She drew her cutlass and adopted a fighting position but relaxed a second later when the face of Skop Groggen appeared over the side. Daniel offered him a hand and the old wizard climbed aboard. His ever present grin hadn't been removed by his ordeal.

"Well, that's enough excitement for one day."

Skop Groggen tipped his head to the side. A small fish flopped out of his ear onto the deck."

"I have to say, though, I don't like that Captain Ironskull. He's spoiled a perfectly good uniform. Oh, and a perfectly good ship. I don't think Captain Firebeard will be too happy either. What a rotter he is, I think I owe him one."

Captain Crimson looked towards the island where the mechanical pirates had vanished.

"As do I. He didn't even have the manners to call me Captain."

Chapter 8: The Oracle

Captain Firebeard was pulled from the water, red faced and angry. He roared about revenge and waved his fist. A shaken George was also pulled to safety, along with several other mariners. They stood, shivering, on the deck. Daniel tried to move towards George but there were too many other people in the way. Captain Crimson stood close to the rescued men; she grinned towards Captain Firebeard.

"Will someone fetch some dry clothes for Captain Firebeard please? He's dripping all over my deck and a man as fashionable as him won't want to be seen with seaweed and salt water all over his outfit."

Before Captain Firebeard could reply, everyone was distracted by a loud thud. Daniel spun around to see what had happened; behind him, someone had fallen, unconscious, to the deck.

It was Owen.

Boulder strode over to the fallen crew member.

"Get up."

He lifted the unconscious man to his feet. Daniel was shocked; it was no longer Owen. The man shook his head, as if waking up.

"What happened?"

Boulder slapped him on the back of the head.

"You fainted. Too much hard work for you, you idle pig."

Suddenly, Daniel felt faint. He took two steps backwards, and sat down with his back to the mast.

The next thing he knew, his mum was shaking him awake in his bedroom. Owen was standing next to his own mother, looking stunned. George was still asleep. Daniel's mum shook her head as he came to his senses.

"You boys, all falling asleep. Where has all your youthful energy gone?"

Owen's mum looked cross.

"I think there's something fishy about this, Owen. Come on, we're going now."

With that, Owen was steered downstairs. Daniel's mum went with them; Daniel stayed upstairs, to wake George. After a second or two of gentle shaking, his friend woke up.

"Daniel? How long have you been back?"

Daniel shrugged.

"A few minutes. Did anything interesting happen after I left?"

"No. A bit of arguing between the pirate captains but not a lot else. The Admiral insisted that they had a mission to complete, so they sailed on."

Daniel walked to the door.

"I'm going downstairs to get a drink."

Nothing more was said about the world of the pirates.

The next day was Saturday. After lunch, Daniel went to see Uncle Alexander at the bookshop. He found his uncle sitting amongst several boxes of old books.

"I've had a delivery, I'm just sorting them out. There are some interesting books here, although not as interesting as "Pirates of the Blood Sea." I expect that's why you've come to see me, isn't it?"

Daniel nodded. Uncle Alexander stood.

"Let's have a cup of tea and a chat."

They moved several piles of books off the seats in the small tea room and Uncle Alexander made two cups of watery tea in a pair of chipped mugs. Uncle Alexander blew across the top of the mug to cool his tea as Daniel enthused about the book. Inevitably, he soon had questions for his uncle.

"Do you know how the map decides which character you're going to be when you enter their world?"

Uncle Alexander was stumped by the question.

"To be honest, I don't know. I'd always assumed you appeared as the same character, whoever you were."

Daniel shook his head.

"That's impossible. How would that work with more than one person going into their world?"

Uncle Alexander sat bolt upright, his eyes wide.

"More than one? That should never happen! Didn't I tell you, only use the map when nobody else is about. I hope you haven't mentioned it to anyone else and if you have, I suggest you tell them that you made it all up. Don't even think about showing anyone else."

Daniel suddenly felt scared.

"Why is that so important?"

His uncle frowned and looked down. He paused for a long time, choosing his words with care when he spoke.

"Daniel, this is not just a story; it's moving between two worlds. Everyone who makes the journey changes things in both this world and the other. Letting too many people across could be dangerous."

Daniel felt sick.

"Dangerous? Why?"

Uncle Alexander sipped his tea.

"Everyone who goes across changes things in ways which can't be undone. That's why only one at a time should go, to make sure the changes are small. I'm not sure exactly what would happen but whoever you're tempted to take with you Daniel, don't."

Daniel went home as soon as he had finished his tea. Worry was growing inside him like stomach ache. He rushed upstairs and picked up the book. He wasn't sure what he expected to see there but the story carried on from where he had left it. Settling into the chair by the window, he started to read.

The Island of Thunder was a giant black rock, hundreds of feet high, surrounded by threatening clouds of darkness; flickering lightning provided the only light near the island as the clouds hid the sun. The small fleet sailed towards it. Looking around at the ships, Tom felt as if they were a mischief of mice, tiptoeing across the open floor towards a waiting tomcat. Nobody spoke. Nobody dared. The only sound was the occasional rumble of thunder, a distant growl of warning that the ships refused to heed.

They landed a few minutes later. Tom was among the landing party, along with Captain Crimson, Captain Firebeard, Boulder and Captain Firebeard's Wizard, along with a few others. They had raced to the shore to avoid the Admiral who was in the boat behind but as Skop Groggen was in the boat with him, they knew they would have to wait. Looking back, Skop Groggen was the only one who had a smile on his face. Everyone else was glancing around with nervous eyes, looking for any sign of the Dead Guardians among the bare, black rocks. The lightning lit up the gloom, making the shadows dance and the sailors jump. Skop Groggen jumped ashore and splashed through the shallows to the beach.

"What a lovely island paradise. Shall we pull up some chairs on the beach, and have an evening drink?"

His voice was far too loud for everyone else. Captain Crimson forgot that he was supposed to be a naval officer and hit him with her hat.

"Hush your noise, you'll bring the Dead Guardians straight to us."

Skop Groggen laughed.

"We don't need to worry about them. We have a wizard with us!"

He pointed towards the unfortunate wizard, who looked as if he might wet his pants at any moment. Captain Crimson gave him a withering look.

"Having him as our guide makes me even more worried."

Skop Groggen glanced back at the Admiral, who was walking up the beach. Keeping his voice low, he spoke to Captain Crimson.

"Don't look at my uniform or forget who I am. I'm not worried and nor should you be."

Captain Crimson put her hat back on as the Admiral strode up. He also showed no fear, just his usual level of simmering annoyance.

"I fail to see what useful information will be gained from anyone who chooses to dwell on such a Heavens-forsaken heap of storm blackened stone. We are wasting valuable time here and each of you will pay for it should it prove as useless as I suspect."

Skop Groggen stood next to the Wizard, who was staring in terror around the beach. He looked close to tears. Skop Groggen put a hand on his shoulder.

"What's that? We should go this way?"

The Wizard nodded, allowing Skop Groggen to lead him up the beach towards a path between the rocks. The others followed in various states of nervousness.

The path wound around the central rocky pillar of Thunder Island. They climbed, Skop Groggen helping the old wizard up the more difficult parts, sometimes shouting back comments like "He says to keep going" or "He wants us to climb higher" to the following group. The only signs of life were small, twisted trees and scrubby weeds alongside the path; there was no sign of animal or bird life. Tom didn't like the flickering of the lightning, getting closer all the time as they climbed higher towards the clouds. Even the Admiral had stopped talking, saving his energy for the climb which was becoming steeper with every twist of the path. Tom's foot slipped on a pebble, which flew away into the empty space next to the path. He glanced to his right; the rock dropped away steeply into blackness about a foot away from where he was standing. He looked away and gripping tightly to a small tree, he pulled himself onwards and upwards.

Daniel put the book down for a moment so that he could go to the toilet. As he left his bedroom, he glanced down at the map. The pins were still sitting next to it; his, George's and Owen's. Why, he wondered, were there several pins if only one person was supposed to travel? As he sat on the lavatory, he thought about it more. They couldn't just be spares, surely? Back in his bedroom Daniel looked down at the map. There, in the corner, was the Island of Thunder. The Oracle might be able to help him make sense of the situation and if he wouldn't, perhaps Skop Groggen could.

Daniel pulled a new hair from his head with the familiar spike of pain, tied it around the pin and, aiming for the centre of the island, plunged it into the map.

Daniel woke up lying on a rock, staring up at a man with a Horse's skull for a head. Shouting with fright, Daniel pushed himself backwards. The skull faced man grabbed his foot to stop him escaping.

"Don't struggle, you'll fall."

Daniel looked behind him. He was on a rocky ledge. One inch from his hand was a drop away to an unknown fate; all was darkness below. Daniel pulled his hand back. The skull faced man hauled him to his feet.

"I'll not hurt you, Tom. Or should I call you Daniel?"

Daniel fought his fear.

"Are you a Dead Guardian?"

Laughter came from beneath the skull.

"No. There are no such things. I let that rumour spread to keep people away. Only the wizards know the truth."

Daniel then knew without being told who this must be.

"You're the Oracle!"

A smile crossed the face beneath the skull.

"You are as clever as I thought you'd be. Now come with me, quickly."

The Oracle jumped straight up in the air. For a second Daniel thought he'd vanished until he looked up and saw that the Oracle had grabbed a rope and was climbing towards an overhanging rock. He reminded Daniel of a monkey as his bony arms and legs pulled him upwards. When he got to the top, he looked down.

"Aren't you going to follow me?"

The Oracle's cave was bigger than Daniel had expected. It was right up above the cloud line; Daniel could see out to the ocean across the top of the clouds. The Oracle gave him a tin mug containing something foul smelling.

"I call this "Nearly Tea." It's made from the leaves of a bush that grows on the far side of the island."

Daniel took a sip and almost spat it out in disgust. It was nothing like tea; it tasted like earwax and soap. He looked down to the ledge below the rope.

"Where are the others? Are they coming?"

The Oracle sipped his drink and sat, cross legged on the floor of the cave entrance.

"They're coming up the path on the other side. They'll be very surprised that you're already here, you'd better tell them that you climbed up a secret path you found or something."

At that moment, Daniel heard voices below. Realising that he had little time, he barked out his question.

"My uncle said that more than one person shouldn't come here using the map. What happens if they do?"

Daniel assumed that the Oracle would know about the map. He was right.

"Well, he's right to be worried. This world is not like your world and everyone who comes here changes things about the way this world is. I can't tell you what the changes are that you have made but I can tell you that Captain Ironskull is only here because someone from your world came here and changed things. This is why the balance of things is upset and why I will help your friends… here they are!"

The Oracle jumped to his feet and strode past the cave entrance. A few seconds later he returned, leading Skop Groggen and the old Wizard. Starting with Skop Groggen, he clasped them both in a manly hug.

"Skop Groggen. Rolf Fleppa it's good to see you both."

Skop Groggen grinned, while Rolf Fleppa looked stunned.

"How do you know my name?"

The Oracle snorted.

"Are you a Sea Wizard or not? Of course I know your name."

The rest of the party arrived, out of breath and panting from the climb. The Admiral looked at the Oracle.

"Who are you, and why are you wearing pieces of dead animal on your head?"

The Oracle smiled.

"Percy, it's good to see you. Now, do you want me to tell you how to fight Captain Ironskull or shall we stand here and discuss my hat all afternoon?"

Even the Admiral sat and listened as the Oracle spoke. Several more tin mugs of Nearly Tea were handed round, although several were soon knocked over "by accident". The Oracle removed the skull once everyone was sitting in his cave but his natural face looked just as odd; his skin was like old leather, his nose was long and crooked while his was hair wild and grey, sprouting in all directions. The light from the small fire flickered across the lines on his face, making it look even more weathered and ancient. He started by telling them what he knew about their situation.

"So, you're all worried about this Captain Ironskull. He's attacking pirates and navy ships as well as merchants and none of you can beat him. You're all worried that he's invincible and that he's going to make sailing impossible across the whole Blood Sea. You want to know how he manages to appear and disappear at will and how he can be beaten. Is that right?"

Captain Crimson put her full mug down on the far side of Captain Firebeard's empty one.

"That's about it. We need to know how we can sink his thrice accursed floating chamber pot."

Captain Firebeard picked up the mug and took a swig. Wincing at the foul taste, he swallowed the vile liquid down.

"Captain Crimson is right. I owe him a sinking."

The Admiral started to recover his wits.

"I have no idea how this man knows so much about us, but I suggest that basic research would undoubtedly be a more likely answer than mystical powers. It takes more than a mountaintop cave and a dead animal atop the head to convince me. I expect to hear some useful information if I am to be convinced that this man is anything other than a fraud."

The Oracle carried on as if nothing had happened.

"Captain Ironskull is able to sneak up on you because his ship is able to travel under the water."

"Impossible! This man is talking utter nonsense!"

The Admiral was unable to contain himself. Daniel shook his head and spoke up.

"No, there are ways it can be done."

"What do you know of it? A cabin boy on a pirate vessel seeks to lecture me on the ways of the sea? Such a vessel would not be able to propel itself. There is no wind beneath the sea and holes for oars would cause a vessel to be flooded. It is impractical nonsense."

Daniel felt squashed but Skop Groggen leaned across to the Admiral and whispered something. The Oracle looked Daniel in the eye as he spoke.

"This boy knows; it is possible. Captain Ironskull is using steam to power his ship. He has fortified Steamhead Island and to defeat him, you must attack him there. If you have struggled to sink his ship, you will have three times the trouble if you try to attack the island. Yet that is what you will have to do if you want to defeat him."

Captain Firebeard jumped to his feet.

"Then tell us what we must do! I want to get on and give him a bloody nose!"

Captain Crimson laughed at her pirate colleague.

"What, do you think it's going to be as easy as sailing to the island and opening fire? Whatever it is that can defeat Captain Ironskull, it's not going to be easy. We're going to need a plan."

The Oracle agreed.

"It will be difficult and nothing I can tell you will make it easier or protect you. It will probably end in your deaths. However, there is one thing that might help you."

The Admiral looked at the Oracle.

"No doubt the aid we seek is only available from a ship made of stone, which flies above the clouds on wings made from mermaid scales."

The Admiral forgot himself and took a big swig of Nearly Tea when he finished talking. The resulting coughing fit hid the giggles and smirking from all the pirates. The Oracle ignored the interruption. Looking out to sea through the cave entrance, he spoke as much to himself as to the group who sat in his cave.

"You must raise the Leviathan."

Chapter 9: The Plan

"Let me understand this clearly. We sail to Doom Atoll and spill some blood on the sand. Then we sail to the island that this metal faced lunatic has fortified, sing a song and a sea monster will destroy it for us? That is your plan, am I correct?"

It was Sunday morning and Daniel was reading the book again. The Oracle had refused to tell the secret of the Leviathan to any except the wizards; Skop Groggen had remained with the Oracle by claiming that Rolf Fleppa would need help to get back down to the beach. Daniel had returned to the ship with the rest of the shore party and had fallen asleep in a hammock before the Wizards returned. Now he was reading about the Admiral's angry response to the Oracle's suggestion. The Admiral, not keen on the supernatural at the best of times, let everyone know how he felt as he addressed the assembled officers.

"Enough time has been wasted on superstition. I suggest that we concentrate our efforts on a military solution. This foolish tale of mythological undersea behemoths, told to us by a ragged, unwashed hermit will not win us naval battles as well you know."

Captain Firebeard, still in a foul mood from losing his ship, rounded on the Admiral with surprising ferocity.

"I wish you'd shut up. All I hear from you is moaning. You cry and whine like a baby, telling us how useless our plans are but you never offer any ideas of your own. The only one here who has made any form of sacrifice is me; I've given my ship in this war. These wizards and the Oracle have provided us with a way to attack Ironskull and your navy has provided us with nothing but your hot air. Say something helpful or shut your bilge hole."

There was silence. The Admiral turned to face Captain Firebeard with a dreadful certainty, like a cannon being turned to fire. To the surprise of the naval officers, he spoke in a calm voice and asked a question.

"You mention wizards. I see only one wizard. Are there others?"

The Admiral looked around the ship, as the pirates exchanged nervous glances. Skop Groggen was nowhere to be seen. Captain Crimson changed the subject.

"What we need is a middle way. We have our information from the Oracle and we should use it but we will also need a plan of attack. The Oracle himself told us that it would be difficult."

"And likely to end in our deaths."

A grinning Skop Groggen stepped out from behind the Admiral, who scowled.

"This is precisely why we must concentrate our efforts on planning rather than chasing around the seas in search of lunatics and monsters."

Captain Crimson looked at the Admiral.

"Shall we vote on it?"

Daniel put the book down and went to get some food.

The next morning, George was waiting outside school.

"Hi Daniel."

"Hi."

They walked across the playground in silence, until George asked a question out of nowhere;

"Have you read any more of the book?"

Daniel glanced across at his friend.

"I read it bit."

George pressed the point.

"Did they find the Oracle? Did they say how Captain Ironskull might be defeated?"

Daniel opened the door to the school. They were early; nobody else was there yet. Daniel shrugged, trying to make it all sound a bit dull.

"There were a few ideas."

George waited, almost jumping up and down in excitement.

"Go on."

Daniel sighed.

"The Oracle said Captain Ironskull has an island fortress. We could use the Leviathan to attack it."

George held the door open, still excited. Daniel walked into the empty classroom.

"When are we going back again? Tonight after school?"

Daniel knew that he ought to say that they weren't, that only one person at a time was supposed to cross to the pirate world and that he couldn't take George with him again. He chickened out.

"I don't know; tonight's not good. I'm, erm, busy. I'll let you know."

Daniel steered the conversation away from pirates or the book for the rest of the day. He slunk away at the end of school, then ran home before George could catch up with him. He felt bad about avoiding and deceiving his friend but put it out of his mind as he climbed the stairs to his bedroom and pulled out the map. He looked down, his eyes darting among the islands, searching for Doom Atoll. It took some time to find as it was very small and near the corner, away from any other islands. Daniel felt the familiar tweak of pain as he pulled out a hair, tied it to the pin and pushed it into the map.

Daniel woke with his face on the sand. It was hot. Not pleasant warmth, but the type of still, oppressive heat which tells of a coming thunderstorm; the type of heat which makes clothes damp, which makes the inside of your head throb and which makes even the smallest movement a great effort. Daniel picked himself up. Grey slabs of threat loomed on the horizon, storm clouds advancing towards them with an inevitable tread. Walking towards him across the sand were five figures, still too far away to recognise. Behind them were a fleet of ships, lying at anchor. Daniel set off walking towards the figures.

"How on earth did you get here ahead of us?"

Captain Firebeard strode up to Daniel; for a moment, he thought that the giant pirate was going to pick him up and shake him.

"I was quick. I ran."

Captain Crimson stepped alongside Captain Firebeard

"Only five of us got into the boat. Did you take a boat of your own?"

She had been a few paces behind Captain Firebeard, with The Admiral and the Wizards a few paces further back. Rolf Fleppa was carrying a dead chicken. A bead of sweat slid down Daniel's neck.

"Well, I…"

Skop Groggen rescued him.

"I asked him to take a raft, come here earlier and prepare things. The wizard told us that he needed a pit dug."

He turned to Daniel.

"Have you done it?"

Daniel shook his head.

"You didn't give me a spade."

A spade was found for Daniel and he was set to work digging. Rolf became very bossy, demanding that the pit be square, with steep sides; every time some sand fell away, the scrawny wizard made Daniel put it right. The heat made him irritable; he was sure that the wizard was making things up just to boss him around. The sun had dipped below the rim of the pit by the time Rolf Fleppa was satisfied with Daniel's work, allowing him to climb out. He looked down into the pit.

"That'll have to do I suppose."

Daniel felt like punching him. Everyone else was sitting around a small fire nearby, drinking something from a dirty bottle. Seeing that he'd finished digging, Skop Groggen wandered over.

"Finished, then? Are we ready for the ritual?"

Rolf Fleppa nodded slowly.

"It is time."

The dead chicken was placed into the hole with a slow seriousness that might've seemed funny if Rolf Fleppa hadn't just made him spend hours digging. The clouds were still lurking, closer but not yet overhead; thunder rumbled around as the chicken was laid to rest but nobody paid it any attention. Daniel didn't like it at all; he wanted to run away and be somewhere else. The scrawny wizard filled in the hole with a few swift swings of the shovel, then turned to the assembled group.

"Now we should sing."

Rolf Fleppa began to drone in a reedy voice. The words sounded like nonsense to Daniel. Clearly he was not the only one to think so; the Admiral opened his mouth to speak but Skop Groggen cut him off.

"Join in as best you can. The more voices, the better, or so I'm told."

With that, he added his voice to Rolf's. Skop Groggen had a clear tenor voice which weaved harmonies around his fellow wizard, turning his droning into the foundation for a haunting refrain. The tune repeated itself even if the words didn't and soon all of the others were joining in, humming along to the unknowable words. Even the Admiral sang along, his deep and resonant voice adding another layer to the sound. After a few moments, Daniel noticed that the sky was dark and the wind was flicking his hair; the black clouds were overhead but where they had been advancing they now swirled like water in a plughole, forming a vortex overhead. Lightning flickered within the swirling mass but no thunder interrupted the song. The tune grew louder and faster and as it did, the clouds swirled faster until, with a long high note that was almost a roar, the song ended. There was a moment of silence before Skop Groggen spoke.

"The blood is in the sand and the song is complete."

As if reminded of his lines in a play, Rolf Fleppa repeated the words.

"Ah, yes. The blood is in the sand and the song is complete."

There was silence. Daniel broke it.

"Now what do we do?"

As he finished speaking, a massive thunderclap boomed like a cannon as lightning smashed into the sand at the far end of the island. Skop Groggen glanced towards the ship, some way off in the opposite direction.

"Now we run."

They ran. None of them looked back, none of them cared about anyone but themselves as they pounded across the sand, rain streaking their faces and stinging their eyes. Captain Crimson ran fastest, followed by Daniel; he didn't know who was next behind him and he didn't care. Their backs were lit by flashes of lightning as the storm gathered force behind them. The boat was thirty paces ahead, then twenty, then ten as he overtook Captain Crimson. Another bolt of lightning struck the sand as Daniel jumped into the boat. Seconds later, the vessel swung back and forth in the water as the others piled in.

The assembled crews stood on the deck of HMS Cantankerous and looked towards the island and the approaching boat. The storm stayed over the island, spectacular displays of forked lightning illuminating the sand below the swirling clouds. In the boat, everyone rowed hard towards the fleet.

"Where's the Leviathan?"

Daniel's question was on everyone's mind but nobody else dared to ask it. Skop Groggen laid a hand on his shoulder.

"It will only arrive when we complete the last step of the ritual. Don't worry. It's not going to rise up and eat us."
He paused with a grin.

"Not yet."

They climbed out of the small boat and were helped aboard the flagship. The journey back to the ship had been terrifying but the fear had eased as they realised that the storm wasn't following them. Now they looked back at the rain lashed isle, the wind making the ropes twitch and ruffling their hair but nothing more. The Admiral, still annoyed by his undignified run across the island, interrogated the wizard as soon as he was on deck.

"Why did that infernal storm spring up? Was it your doing?"

Rolf Fleppa began stuttering, so Skop Groggen stepped in.

"It's part of the ritual. Summoning up the Leviathan also acts like a storm ritual."

The Admiral rounded on him.

"You know an awful lot about it, Mr Church. Why exactly is this?"

The Admiral scowled at him. Skop Groggen had a reply ready.

"I've been listening to this wizard. After all, knowledge is power, is that not so, sir?"

The Admiral grunted a dismissive snort.

"You can fill your head will as much nonsense as you like, Mr Church. I doubt you'll find yourself more powerful for it. Now bring me a greatcoat before I catch my death of cold."

Daniel woke up shortly after, pleased to escape the storm and the wind. After shivering on deck for a few minutes, he had been glad when Captain Firebeard had suggested that they all needed to go below and have a tot of rum. Daniel had climbed down through the hatch and sat down with the others; exhaustion caused him to nod off in no time.

He used the chair next to his bed to help him stand up. He yawned, stepped forward and almost fell over George.

This was a surprise; his friend, lying on the floor of his bedroom. It took a second or two for Daniel to remember; George hadn't been with him when he used the map, nor had George come to Doom Atoll. Daniel glanced across at the map. His own pin was once again lying beside the map. He looked at the map; in a few seconds he had found George's pin.

It was stuck into Steamhead Island.

Chapter 10. The Gathering Storm

"What were you doing?"

Daniel fought to control his anger. George had taken a few seconds to wake but was now standing face to face with Daniel.

"I was looking for you."

Daniel shook his head.

"Who said you could come in and use my map?"

Daniel was angry, partly because George had used the map without asking but also because of Uncle Alexander's warning; Daniel knew it was serious and now the rules had been broken again. Daniel knew that he would be blamed if his uncle found out, whether it was his fault or not. George held his hands up in a gesture of peace.

"Hey, calm down. I was only looking for you. After last time, I thought you'd need all the help you can get."

Daniel hadn't calmed down. He picked up the map and held it to his chest, as if George might try to take it from him.

"How did you get in here?"

George gestured towards the door.

"I knocked on the door and your mum let me in, like she usually does when I call by. I don't see why it's a big deal."

Daniel put the map behind his back.

"Ok, so why weren't you with us? Why did you go to Steamhead Island?"

George stammered his reply; he seemed to be surprised by the question.

"What do you mean?"

Daniel pressed the matter, being more aggressive than he would usually due to his anger.

"Your pin was stuck into Steamhead Island. Why?"

George was flustered and his reply was blurted out.

"I was looking for you."

Daniel, unconvinced, pointed to the pins on the table.

"So why didn't you put your pin where mine was?"

George looked at the floor.

"I didn't think of that."

Daniel snorted and turned towards the door. He was tired of the whole situation and felt hungry.

"Come on, let's go and get some food."

George had discovered two things about Steamhead Island. First, it was a volcano; Daniel already knew this. Second, a wooden gate was being built across the harbor which guarded the entrance to the fortress. Daniel had hardly spoken to George until they had eaten some toast; after that, he had calmed down enough to discuss the pirate world. The information was useful; George had appeared in the rocky area high above the fortress and managed to look down at the back of the fortress gate.

"It's wooden, and looks as if it's held in place with two huge chains. That way they can raise it when they need to."

Daniel was puzzled.

"Captain Ironskull uses metal to build everything. Why would he use wood for the gate?"

George shrugged.

"No idea, mate. I didn't think it was a good idea to go and ask him. I just saw what I saw."

"You're certain it was wood?"

George nodded.

"It was wood alright. The gate was made of big thick timbers, each as thick as a tree trunk."

Daniel sat back in his chair, eating his toast.

"It has to be a weak point, surely?"

George finished his mouthful, then replied.

"They were thick beams. Maybe he wants to protect it from rust or perhaps he's run out of metal."

Daniel wasn't convinced but let the matter drop. The pirates weren't discussed for the rest of the afternoon.

The next day, Daniel went to see Uncle Alexander. While his conversation with George had taken away most of the ill feeling, it had done nothing to ease his worries about other people going to the pirate world. Now George had used the map without his knowledge or permission, he felt safer telling his uncle about it. As soon as school was over, Daniel went straight to the bookshop. It gave him a good excuse to avoid taking George back to his house with him but he still felt a twinge of guilt as he dodged away at the end of school, giving his friend the slip in the crowd of children crossing the playground.

As ever, his uncle started by putting the kettle on. Two or three people were browsing in the shop but Uncle Alexander left them to it so he could make the tea. After the last of the customers had paid and left, Uncle Alexander pulled up some chairs.

"So, my boy. What can I do for you? Have you finished the book already?"

Daniel sipped his tea. It was still too hot; it burned his mouth and made his tongue feel furry.

"No, not yet. I wanted to talk to you about what you said the other day."

Uncle Alexander looked at him over the rim of his teacup.

"Which bit exactly?"

The look made Daniel nervous. It felt as if his uncle knew what he wanted to say and was waiting for him to say it. Daniel took a long breath in and spoke before his courage deserted him.

"The bit about other people coming with me to the pirate world."

Uncle Alexander's expression didn't change.

"Go on."

Daniel blurted out his confession.

"My friend found his way into pirate world. I didn't ask him to but he followed me there. I didn't know he'd done it until I found him asleep in my bedroom with a pin stuck in the map."

Uncle Alexander sipped his tea and asked a question in a calm voice.

"How did he find out how to use the map and the pins?"

Daniel's reply was sheepish.

"I might've told him about that."

Uncle Alexander put his teacup down and placed his fingers together in front of him.

"I think you should tell me everything."

Daniel told Uncle Alexander about Daniel coming with him to the world of the pirates, about how he invited George to go with him, about how his friend became a naval officer and about how, following the warning Uncle Alexander gave, he tried to put him off, but George followed him anyway.

However, Daniel didn't mention Owen; confessing to taking two people into the pirate world with him was just too much to admit to, especially with one of them being one of the bullies. Uncle Alexander listened in silence until Daniel had finished. After a pause that seemed to last for weeks, Uncle Alexander gave his opinion.

"Well, it can't be denied that you have been foolish. You were told that only one person should travel using the map yet you ignored this. However, from the sounds of things, there hasn't been too much damage yet. You are right to stop your friend coming with you again and should keep the map and book to yourself from now on."

"Damage?"

Daniel didn't like the sound of that. His uncle explained.

"As you were told before, using the map lets you into the world of the pirates and everyone who goes across changes things in ways which can't be undone. Do you understand what the book and map are?"

Daniel answered as best he could.

"The map is a way of getting into the book."

Uncle Alexander was becoming excited again, talking more quickly as he explained.

"You're almost right but I think you're missing one important detail. It's easiest if I show you, I think. Have you got the book with you?"

Daniel reached into his bag; he had brought the book with him, and he pulled it out. Uncle Alexander took it from him.

"Have you looked at the future chapters? Have you seen what it says later on?"

Daniel thought about it for a second and realised he hadn't. He told his uncle this.

"I looked a page or so ahead but no more than that."

"Look now."

Uncle Alexander handed the book back. Daniel took it. He held it in his hands. Uncle Alexander prompted him.

"Turn to the back."

Daniel did so. The back page was blank, as was the next to last page, and the one before that. Daniel flicked backwards; the pages were all blank, right the way back to the events on Doom Atoll. Daniel looked at his uncle.

"They're blank."

His uncle nodded. Daniel continued.

"How am I supposed to read the next pages of the book if it's blank?"

Uncle Alexander shook his head in frustration.

"You still don't understand?"

Daniel felt annoyed. He didn't understand and felt as if his uncle was trying to test or tease him. He kept the frustration out of his voice and forced himself to speak calmly.

"No, I don't understand. What are you trying to tell me?"

Uncle Alexander was almost exploding with excitement.

"Daniel, you aren't using the map to get into a book which has already been written. You're using the map to get into another world; the book is recording what happens!"

Daniel thought about it for a moment.

"You mean, nobody wrote the book? It's recording actual events somewhere?"

Uncle Alexander sipped his tea.

"Yes."

There was a long pause as Daniel tried to take this in.

"Where?"

Uncle Alexander finally cracked a wry, knowing smile.

"Pirate world."

Shortly after, Uncle Alexander turned serious again.

"That's why you can't take too many people there. Everyone who goes changes that world and once a change is made, it cannot be undone. I know that things changed when I went there."

Uncle Alexander paused, looking into his teacup for a few seconds before speaking again.

"It's important that there isn't too much change."

Daniel was interested by this.

"Why?"

Uncle Alexander thought before speaking.

"You always have a choice; you can read the next pages in the book, in which case things happen without you, like a normal book. Alternatively you can use the map, in which case you join in with events. When you join in, you help decide how things will turn out, just like in our world. This is why you have to be careful. Every action has consequences."

Over the rest of the cup of tea, Daniel learned as much as Uncle Alexander knew about the world of the pirates. Where exactly the world was he didn't know but it was a world where ships were still mostly powered by sail, where technology was very limited and where things which he took for granted, such as mobile phones and submarines were unheard of. Daniel already knew all this from having been there. Things got more interesting when his uncle told him about the sea monsters.

"They're real, Daniel. Very real, and they aren't something to be messed around with. If the pirates have tried to summon one, then they're in a lot of danger."

"Why?"

Uncle Alexander looked at him as if he was stupid.

"It's a monster, Daniel. We aren't just talking about something you can put on a lead and take for a walk. It's called a monster for a reason. If they think it'll do what they tell it to just because they ask it nicely, they're in for a big shock."

Daniel left shortly after that, following a final warning to keep the book to himself. The sun was setting over the fields behind the footpath as he climbed over the gate which led to the main road. His heart sank in his chest as he saw Bill, Barry and Owen waiting by the bus stop on the other side of the road. He thought about turning round and sneaking away but Bill had seen him.

"Hey, look, it's the bookworm."

Daniel dropped over the far side of the gate into the road. He tried to sound casual.

"Hi guys."

Barry walked across the road. Daniel tried to walk away but Bill stood in his way. Barry made a grab for the bag but missed.

"What's in the bag, wimp?"

Daniel walked around Bill and carried on up the lane.

"Just my school things. Nothing you'd want and I'm off home now anyway."

Barry made a second grab at the bag, this time pulling it off Daniel's shoulder. It caught his arm and spun him around. Daniel tried to pull away but the bully was bigger and stronger. He wrestled the bag away, pulled the zip open, turned it upside down and threw the contents into the road.

"It's just a load of books. Nothing useful."

Bill caught up. He saw Daniel's PE kit lying in the road.

"Let's teach the little wimp how to play football."

Bill kicked Daniel's maths book up the road. It landed in a puddle. Barry laughed and picked up another book as Daniel tried to gather his things from the road before a car came.

"Rugby time. Let's see if we can score a drop goal."

Owen finally caught up with them.

"Hey, Barry. Throw me the book."

Barry threw the book; Owen grabbed it out of the air.

"Go on Owen, see if you can get it over the hedge."

Owen looked at Daniel with his familiar sneer of contempt. He glanced down at the book and was about to say something cruel to Daniel when he stopped and read the title.

"Pirates of the Blood Sea."

He looked back at Daniel. His expression changed.

"What book is this?"

Daniel looked up from the road, with his arms full of school books.

"I think you know."

Owen tossed it gently onto the verge. He looked away from Daniel and walked away up the road.

"Come on lads, he's not worth the effort."

With a shrug, Bill and Barry followed him away into the gloom. Daniel gathered up his things and stuffed them into his bag. Last of all, he picked up the pirate book; glancing up the road, the three bullies were already out of sight among the shadows.

Chapter 11: Into the Maelstrom

Daniel clumped up the stairs as soon as he got home and checked the contents of his bag. Nothing was missing, which was a mercy; the only book which was damaged was the maths book which had landed in the puddle. Daniel put it by the radiator to dry, then examined the Pirates book. It was fine. Sitting down on the bed, he flipped it open and began to read.

The Admiral had been in much better spirits since the military planning began. He held court over the assembled Captains and crew, organising and commanding with his usual blustery manner but with new energy and pride. Captain Firebeard bristled with barely concealed irritation as the Admiral pointed at the map and gave his instructions for the third time that morning.

"You, Captain Firebeard, will run HMS Oppressive line astern to my flagship, HMS Cantankerous, until I give the order to sail forward and fire at any defences on the island. You will obey my commands at all times as a ship of the line; remember, the ship is placed under your command only because I say so, you are not a part of the navy and you will account for any losses…"

"You've told me all that before, Percy."

The Admiral ignored the use of his first name, which annoyed Captain Firebeard even more. He was about to say something even more insulting when Skop Groggen, dressed in his naval uniform and standing beside the Admiral, turned the conversation back to the plan by pointing at the map.

"So, the main fleet will strike here, at the heart of the island once any defences have been destroyed by the Leviathan."

The Admiral shook his head.

"As I have said many times, we will strike the defences down in a coordinated military attack. This will be effective when the undersea monstrosity fails to arrive and you realise that it is no more than superstition and fairy tales. I am surprised, Mr Church, that you have been taken in by such nonsense. Clearly, you have spent too much time with that wizard."

Captain Crimson smirked at the Admiral.

"When you've finished your little squabble, do you think we could get back to planning our suicide mission? It's bad enough that I have to sail into certain death, it makes it so much worse if I have to sail into certain death alongside old men that are always squabbling like toddlers who all want the same dolly."

The Admiral turned towards Captain Crimson and roared with sudden anger.

"You will remember your place! I am the commander of the King's Navy and I will not tolerate this…"

Skop Groggen cut him off by pointing to the map again, and to the model ships arranged around Steamhead Island.

"So, to confirm our plan. The fleet will line up as we have placed them here, we will hit these targets in sequence and should the Leviathan fail to turn up, it will be Captain Firebeard in the Oblivious who takes on that task. Each of us knows our part in the plan. We are agreed on this?"

There was a seconds pause, then everyone present responded with a shout.

"Aye!"

A knock on the door disturbed Daniel's reading. He put the book down on the bed and trotted down the stairs. His spirits fell as he opened the door; it was George.

"Hi."

"Hi."

Daniel stood, facing his friend.

"Are you going to invite me in?"

Daniel's brain raced, thinking of a reason to refuse.

"I can't. I'm, erm… busy."

George stayed in place, not moving.

"Busy doing what?"

Daniel felt annoyed.

"Homework."

George snorted.

"We haven't got any homework that's due tomorrow."

"I like to get it done early."

"No you don't. You sometimes do it on the bus on the way to school. Anyway, I only want to come in for a minute."

Daniel wished that he'd never started the discussion. He motioned towards the living room.

"Come on then. I'll have a break for a little while and do the rest of my work later. We can have some lemonade and watch a film."

George had no interest in watching a film. As soon as he was inside, he started talking about the pirate world.

"So, when are we going to use the map again?"

Daniel shook his head. He was annoyed enough to tell George what he should've said before without feeling bad about it.

"We aren't. It's not a game. We have to stop it."

Daniel expected George to complain. George did exactly that.

"I know it's not a game, I'm not stupid, but we have to help in the battle. You know they need our help."

"I think the pirates and the navy will be able to fight their own battle without a load of kids getting involved."

George put his lemonade down.

"Why is it so bad if we use the map, anyway?"

Daniel snapped his reply.

"It's dangerous."

This was impossible to argue with, Daniel thought; after all, George had almost been killed by Captain Ironskull.

"So we aren't going to go back just because it's a bit dangerous?"

Daniel didn't have a chance to reply; the sound of the key in the front door interrupted them. As he stood and turned, he saw his mum coming in. alongside her was Owen and his mum.

"We can't do it again, it's dangerous."

Daniel had been told by his mum that the three boys would have to go upstairs to play while the two ladies had their meeting in the living room. What had been a difficult situation with George had now turned into a nightmare as both George and Owen wanted to use the map and Owen wouldn't take no for an answer. Daniel's protests fell on deaf ears; while George was persistent, Owen was a bully who didn't care about hurting Daniel's feelings or damaging his things.

"Why don't we just get the map out anyway? We know how to use it and the little cabin boy here isn't strong enough to stop us."

George didn't look happy but he did nothing to stop Owen from picking up the pins next to the map. He was already tying his hair onto the pin when Daniel thought of something.

"You don't know where to go."

Owen paused, pin in hand.

"What do you mean?"

"You don't know where the ships are, where the story has got to. Only I know where the ships have sailed to and what has happened in the story. If you put the pins in somewhere else, it'll do you no good."

Owen was confused.

"What are you on about? What story?"

Daniel shook his head.

"That's for me to know."

Owen clenched his fist.

"How many times will I have to punch you before you tell me?"

Daniel looked across at George. George stood stone still, eyes wide with fear.

"Perhaps you should just tell him. It would be easier wouldn't it?"

Owen's eyes had been looking around the room. As they passed over the bed, he smiled the sort of smile a cat might give a mouse.

"This book of yours, the old pirate book. That's going to tell me what I need to know, isn't it?"

He picked it up

"Or perhaps I should just start ripping pages out, one by one, until you tell me?"

Daniel was defeated and he knew it. Keeping the book undamaged was more important than keeping people out of pirate world.

"Ok, you win. We can use the map. We'll need to go to Steamhead Island but you'll have to listen to me before we do."

Daniel told them about the planned attack on Steamhead Island. Owen grew more excited as Daniel explained while George looked more and more worried.

"We can't start on Steamhead Island; that's where Captain Ironskull is. We need to join the ships which are attacking. How do we do that?"

Daniel shook his head.

"We can't. It's impossible. We can only put the pins on land."

"Why?"

Owen's earlier bullying had been replaced by a puppy like excitement. Daniel explained.

"If we appear in the sea, we will probably drown. The map is small, the sea is huge and we don't know exactly where the ships are."

George joined in.

"If we know the attack is about to start, we can either appear on the ships or be close enough to swim to them."

"The map covers a huge area; we could appear miles away."

Owen picked his pin up.

"You're just trying to put us off again."

"No, I'm serious. I was told that we must never…"

Daniel's sentence was never completed as Owen jabbed his pin into the sea near Steamhead Island.

Daniel kicked the chair in frustration.

"For crying out loud. He's an idiot!"

George looked at the map.

"Do we try to rescue him?"

Daniel sighed.

"We have to."

Picking up their pins, Daniel and George stuck them into the map touching Owen's, hoping that they wouldn't all be lost in the vast, sweeping ocean.

The shock of cold water was the first thing that hit Daniel. He plunged down into the sea, going under then bobbing to the surface. Huge waves surrounded him on all sides, like mountains of water. He struggled to breathe, gasping hard as another wave lifted him high and smashed him down hard, pushing him under again. This time Daniel was able to hold his breath and as he surfaced, he took a huge gulp of air. The waves lifted him again; this time he was able to make out two things as he rose high in the water; two other people were in the water nearby; Daniel assumed that they were George and Owen. The second thing he noticed was a collection of sails ahead of them; they looked a long way off but Daniel knew that they must be the ships and he had to reach them. He started to swim.

He caught up with George and Owen within five minutes; they said few words to each other, saving their breath and energy for swimming. Sometimes the sea worked with them, pushing them towards the ships but sometimes it swirled them away; at these times it felt as if they were fighting against the whole power of the ocean, a fight they could never win. Daniel knew that if he was going to survive he couldn't give in to despair but already his arms hurt like fire and his legs felt as if they were going to drag him down, they were so heavy. Were the sails closer? It was hard to tell. Another wave rose and fell, plunging the three down into another wave valley. They swam on, insignificant specks in a world of water.

A lifetime seemed to pass as they fought the uncaring sea. Eventually, the sails grew larger, which gave a new burst of energy to the swimmers. A shout went up from the closest ship as they drew close; a rope was thrown over the side for them to climb. Owen was first to reach it and although it took him several minutes, he managed to climb aboard. Daniel was second; he could hardly haul his body out of the water before his arms gave way and plunged him back into the sea. A shout from on board gave him a lifeline;

"Wrap the rope around you, we'll haul you up."

Seconds later, all three were face to face with the Admiral. Daniel cursed his luck; of all the ships to be rescued by, HMS Cantankerous was the worst possible result. The Admiral looked them up and down.

"All three of you are cowards who deserved to drown for deserting your duties."

Owen spoke up.

"We aren't deserters."

A glare from the Admiral made him add the word "sir" to the end of his statement. The Admiral paused before continuing.

"So, you expect me to believe that all three of you were swept overboard, then carried away before you could shout for help? Not only this, all three of you swim back to the ship together, arriving at exactly the same moment?"

George tried to say that this was exactly what had happened but the Admiral talked over the top of him.

"This is what I believe happened, gentlemen. You decided that you would leave your shipmates to risk their lives in the coming battle and that you would try to escape using a raft. You took your raft when all three of you were on watch last night, then tried to sail it away, towards the islands we passed yesterday. When the sea turned rough and sank your raft, you had no choice except swimming back to the ships. Am I correct?"

Daniel thought about telling the truth but instead, chose to remain silent. The Admiral allowed a few seconds to pass, then passed judgement.

"Your silence confirms your guilt. I will decide your punishment in due course. Mr Church, have these men taken to the brig and clapped in irons."

The brig was dark and damp; rats ran around their feet and the irons pinched their flesh. None of them spoke for several minutes until George turned to Daniel and whimpered a question.

"How do we get out of this?"

Daniel pulled his foot away as something wriggled past in the gloom.

"I have no idea."

He could feel Owen's glare despite the darkness.

"Aren't you supposed to know the story? Why don't you tell us what happens next?"

"It isn't like that. I can't see the future here any more than I can at home."

Owen splashed at something in the darkness.

"What about that stupid book? What's written in there?"

Daniel took advantage of the darkness to throw a look of annoyance at the bully.

"It works like a history book. It can't tell the future any more than the history books at school can. Not that you'd know, having never read a book in your life."

Daniel would never have dared to say something so rude to Owen if they hadn't been chained up. Owen said nothing in reply. Daniel was surprised by this and he had plenty of time to ponder it; nothing else was said until they were collected to face the Admiral once more.

The three were taken, still in chains, to stand before an assembly of the pirate captains, the senior officers and the Admiral himself. The setup was familiar to Daniel and George; it was a naval court. The Admiral alone was seated and as they were led in, he stood and spoke to everyone there.

"These three men have tried to run from the coming battle. They would leave each one of you to die while they run to save their worthless skins. We have little time to waste, so I will pass sentence without delay."

Despite this promise, the pause before he spoke lasted ages. Eventually, looking each in the eye in turn, he pronounced judgement.

"While I would willingly hang each of you from the mainmast, we will need every able sailor in the coming battle if we are to stand a chance of victory. Therefore, I have spoken to the pirate captains and we all agree on your punishment. You will be included in most dangerous part of the operation. You will go with Captain Crimson into the jaws of death, as part of the shore landing party."

Chapter 12: The attack begins

"It's too quiet."

Captain Crimson stood on the bow of her ship, looking towards Steamhead Island. The mighty volcano stood in silence, a small cloud of steam the only evidence of it's dangerous power. At the base of the mountain, barely visible, stood two towers and a gate; behind them lurked the stronghold of Captain Ironskull. Daniel tried to be positive.

"Perhaps they don't know we're coming and we can catch them unawares."

Daniel, along with the rest of the shore party, had been moved to the bow of Captain Crimson's ship. The plan hadn't been explained to them; all they knew was that they would have the most difficult and dangerous job, being in the landing party. Captain Crimson replied, her voice quiet.

"I wish I shared your sunny outlook. They know we're coming."

Owen gripped the rail hard, his knuckles white. Daniel could see that he was trying not to shake. Keeping his voice steady, the bully joined the conversation.

"Why would they know we're coming?"

If Captain Crimson knew that he was seeking some hope to cling to, she didn't show it.

"Captain Ironskull always knows where his enemies are. He appears without warning, he disappears like a ghost. He has powers…"

Daniel breathed out slowly, trying to keep his thundering heart under control.

"I hope he doesn't know everything."

Captain Crimson looked at him, an eyebrow raised. Daniel continued,

"Sooner or later we'll have to fight him. I just hope that whatever the plan is, it works and he doesn't know about it."

Captain Crimson looked towards the fortress.

"So do I."

Stage one of the plan relied on stealth and deception. The shore party had to find a way to get to the island without being noticed, and without Captain Ironskull realising who was with them.

"We need him to pay attention to the big ships, while our little boat sneaks by."

Skop Groggen had joined them; Daniel was pleased that he would be part of the shore party, along with Rolf Fleppa. The two wizards would be needed on dry land to summon the Leviathan. Daniel also wondered why Captain Crimson was coming with them rather than staying to command her ship. However, when he asked Skop Groggen, the wizard gave a vague answer.

"This is all you need to know; she will be in charge. Your role will be to pull the oars and scout ahead once we reach the island. The other two will fight off any attacks; Rolf Fleppa will summon the Leviathan with his awesome wizardly power. I'm there for my good looks."

Daniel laughed.

"When are we setting off?"

"As soon as the first cannon fires."

Boulder put on Captain Crimson's spare hat.

"Do you think they'll believe this?"

He was standing next to the lifeboat, where the shore party was preparing to launch. His hat went with the red coat but other than that, he looked nothing like his captain. She looked up at him from the lowering lifeboat.

"Of course they will. Just don't sail too close to them."

Daniel thought that they'd have to sail a very long way away for the disguise to work. He wasn't sure why they needed to disguise someone as Captain Crimson and why Captain Crimson wasn't keeping command of her own ship but still nobody would talk to him about it. He was hushed to silence as the boat reached the water.

"We need to keep as quiet as possible if we're going to make it to shore without being seen."

If he'd wanted to reply, it would've been useless; with a sudden, explosive shock, every cannon on the far side of the ship fired at once, a full broadside. Shouting followed from the deck above, the frantic confusion of sudden battle. Captain Crimson yelled at the party in the boat;

"That's our signal! Pull for shore!"

Captain Crimson's command was obeyed without a word as the boat moved away from the protection of the ship.

The reason for the cannon fire was soon clear; Captain Ironskull had appeared. His ship was on the far side, closer to the island; his turrets whizzing cannonballs towards their ship. Captain Crimson watched from the bench next to Skop Groggen, her hat and coat hidden under a sack.

"Why's he attacking the stern?"

Now that battle was joined, Owen seemed interested in naval tactics. Skop Groggen answered him.

"I think he wants to avoid the broadside. His ship can survive most things but with so many enemies to fight he has to be careful; a full broadside could weaken his ship and leave him trapped out here against every gun we have. He's probably trying to get one ship alone, disable the rudder and take it out of the fight that way before his fortress comes under attack. See, he's keeping to the island side so no other ship can fire at him without hitting their comrades."

Cannonfire was making the water fizz and churn but very few shots were hitting either ship. They watched as they rowed away from the battle; Daniel felt helpless in the open launch, like a mouse running past two fighting cats. While nobody was shooting at them, one stray cannonball would kill them all. Owen pointed as the spray of the waves slapped them in the face, cold and salty; several navy ships were now closing with Captain Ironskull. Soon the fight would be against the whole fleet but they were also approaching the island; soon they would be in range of the massive turrets there too. Rolf Fleppa saw this and shouted over the roar of battle.

"We need to summon the Leviathan. Pull harder!"

Within minutes, they were rounding the island. Daniel was pleased to see the battle fading away but their journey took them close enough to the huge turrets to make him nervous. Each was at least forty feet high, with a metal cone at the top. Out of this protruded a huge cannon, far bigger than a ship could carry. They had looked tiny compared to the mountain but now he was close he could see their size and power. They stood above like iron giants, soulless sentries guarding the seaward approach to the fortress. There was no sign of anyone near them but he knew enough about Captain Ironskull to realise that unseen eyes watched from within those imposing towers. As he looked, Daniel noticed that the gate was made of wood, as George had said. He didn't have time to think about it for long though, as Captain Crimson hissed at him to keep rowing.

No sooner was the boat beached than they were scrambling across the sand dunes and up towards the mountain of fire. Their target was a hill near the back of the fortress; it lacked the height of the mountain but would be high enough for them to see the battle and as importantly, see down into the fortress itself. Captain Crimson took her coat and hat with her as they ran.

"At the crucial time, I'm going to want them to see where I really am."

"When will that be?"

Captain Crimson answered as she ran ahead.

"Just before Captain Ironskull dies."

The hilltop was windy; sand from the dunes whipped into the air and stung their eyes. Looking over the hilltop and down into the bay below, they had a perfect view of the unfolding battle. The ships had moved closer to the fortress but the navy had set their battle line up so that the turrets couldn't fire on them without shooting past their own captain, who in turn risked a full broadside if he tried to attack. Skop Groggen grinned.

"That Admiral knows how to fight a sea battle."

Captain Crimson nodded.

"He's bought you the time you needed. Now get that monster up!"

Skop Groggen turned to Rolf Fleppa.

"Are we going to keep pretending that you're doing all this, or shall I lead?"

Rolf Fleppa shook his head.

"You do it. I'll be the assistant."

Owen and George looked surprised, but neither said anything as Rolf Fleppa reached into a sack and removed a dead chicken.

"You'll want this first."

Daniel glanced away, towards the battle below. The Navy were circling their ships, trying to get as many cannons as possible aiming towards the Iron Ship. Daniel could see the flash of red, which was Boulder dressed as Captain Crimson. From this distance at least, it looked convincing. As he watched, more cannon fire hissed towards the stern of Captain Crimson's ship. Next to him, the two wizards were lighting a driftwood fire and chanting the song from Doom Atoll. Owen pointed towards the battle.

"Look; The Crimson Firedrake is heading for the gate!"

It was true. The ship was sailing towards the island, trying to get close enough to the shore that it could sail to the gate along the coastline, out of range of the turrets. Captain Crimson watched on, her face a tense mask as her ship came under fire from the turrets. The first shots missed. Owen cheered, but Captain Crimson silenced him with a wave of her arm.

"Those shots were just finding their range. They'll be more accurate next time."

The navy were driving a wedge between Captain Ironskull and Captain Crimson's ship. Captain Ironskull was being forced to sail into open water or face the broadside from the fleet; this left Captain Crimson's vessel free to sail towards the gate. A second blast from the left turret whizzed close to the ship, making Captain Crimson flinch.

"At least from that angle, only one turret can fire."

Daniel's words were met with silence from Captain Crimson. The wind moaned across the bare ground, accompanying the chanting. Two more shots whizzed close to the ship, one ripping through the sails. Owen swore.

"They'll be hit for certain next shot!"

Captain Crimson remained silent, facing towards the sea.

Then, two things happened. The chanting stopped as Skop Groggen threw the chicken onto the fire. For a few seconds, there was a churning out at sea, as if something fizzy had been dropped into the ocean. It was further out than the fleet or Captian Ironskull but close enough to be seen by all of them. Then, out of nowhere, clouds gathered. A flash of lightning split the sky, the thunder echoing around them as the churning moved towards the gate, slowly but with clear purpose.

"What on earth is happening there?"

George spoke for the first time. Skop Groggen looked pleased with himself.

"That, young sir, is the Leviathan rising. Keep watching."

They did. Rain started to fall, just light drizzle at first. The turrets, realising that a new danger was approaching, turned in place and fired towards the disturbance. Captain Crimson's ship took advantage of the distraction, sailing straight across the gate and firing a full broadside into it.

"It's split the timbers!"

Daniel couldn't contain his excitement; while there were now defenders visible close to the gate, they couldn't do anything about the blast, nor from the next broadside as the ship put about and let fly from the starboard side. Planks flew in all directions; even from distance, Daniel heard the crash as the cannonballs smashed the wooden gate to pieces. The gate was almost gone, just a few planks still hung in place. The ship turned again, sailing into the gap left by its own firepower. Small flashes lit up, shots being fired back and forth from the defenders on the fortress wall and the pirates on the ship before the side of the mountain and the fortress cut it off from view.

"They've taken the gate!"

Daniel yelled out in triumph, running forward to see through the gate. The churning disturbance was growing bigger, a blue bulge now emerging above the waves. George ran forward.

"Look, the monster is following."

The back of the ship was clearing the gateway, the defenders on the wall scattering as the ship sailed into their harbour. Glancing out to sea, Daniel saw that the Leviathan was getting bigger; malevolent red eyes glowed from the front of the bulge. As they watched, the churning in front of the beast gave way to a mass of tentacles, grasping and writhing towards their prey. George gasped.

"It's a giant octopus."

"It looks more like a squid to me."

Skop Groggen peered down a tiny brass telescope towards the monstrosity. Captain Crimson strolled up behind them.

"I'm more interested in what happens to my ship."

She looked past them towards the gate.

"Something's wrong."

Daniel looked at her.

"What is it? What's wrong?"

"It's too easy. We've been fighting Captain Ironskull's ship for months and we've never so much as dented it, while he sinks us at will. Why is it that he suddenly can't hit our ships even once? Why would he leave his own front door so weak? Two knocks and the ship got in. That can't be right. Something's going on."

"Perhaps they just thought the turrets would keep them safe. A wooden gate is quicker and easier to open and close."

Daniel looked back towards the Leviathan. It was getting closer to the fortress; the naval line had used the distraction to follow the beast towards the shore. Daniel was so busy watching them, he didn't see what happened at the gate until Captain Crimson shouted.

"What in the name of…"

Daniel looked at the gate. Steam was rising from the turrets; a shrill whistling which spoke of machines working at the limit of their endurance. Huge chains had snapped tight in the gateway; at first Daniel thought that these must be the trap until he saw that they were moving upwards, pulling something into place from below the water. He saw the ship, still close to the gateway trying to turn in place and escape but the chains moved so swiftly that the sailors had no chance. Daniel saw Boulder waving his arms about on deck, giving frantic orders before the red coat and hat disappeared behind a wall of black steel which shot out of the water into the gap, a second gate made of metal now sealed them in with a boom like thunder. Huge spikes on top pointed towards the sky.

"They're trapped in there!"

More lightning tore the sky across the bay as the storm grew. Captain Crimson sat down on the floor, her hat in her hand. Skop Groggen bent down and said something to her; nobody else could hear what it was. Captain Crimson stood up and walked a few steps away, looking towards the gate. Owen also stood, his eyes fixed on the fortress.

"I don't understand it. Why would they capture them? Why not just sink the ship at sea?"

Skop Groggen peered through his telescope. Unlike everyone else, he looked calm.

"I don't know exactly what they're planning. However, we do have an advantage. Whatever their plan is, it won't work."

Daniel looked at the wizard.

"Why not?"

Skop Groggen grinned.

"They've fallen for our decoy. They think they've captured Captain Crimson."

Chapter 13: The battle for the fortress

The Leviathan ignored the first two shots from the turrets; they missed and splashed harmlessly into the sea. The mass of tentacles churned the water as the great beast neared the shallows of the bay. The fortress fired another volley, missing again but closer now. The naval ships kept their line, tracking the monster from a cautious distance as it closed on the fortress. Owen stared out across the bay, hand shielding his eyes from the sun.

"It's not big enough to break that metal gate, especially with those turrets firing at it. It's going to…"

The sentence died on Owen's lips.

The Leviathan stood up.

A green giant with slime dripping from its huge, muscular body rose from the water, the squid forming the giant's head, the mass of tentacles writhing around the chin of the monster. It towered over the gate and the nearby ships and as it stood, it threw its arms back and gave a gurgling roar, head pointing to the sky. George swore. Skop Groggen nodded to himself.

"That's what I call a monster."

It waded towards the gate with a slow tread, like a man fording a shallow stream. The people in the fortress ran around like ants when their nest has been kicked over. Muskets fired, their shots tiny compared to the massive legs. However, the turrets also fired and now found their mark; a flash of red appeared on the giant's left shin. Seconds later, another red smear appeared, then another. The Leviathan swatted at its leg in obvious pain as blood trickled down, mixing with the sea water.

"We can't stand and watch all day, we've got a job to do!"

George surprised them with his sudden enthusiasm. Skop Groggen walked across to him.

"I have no fear, officer. Our plan's going as it should."

Captain Crimson continued to look across the bay. The turrets were continuing to blast chunks out of the monster's legs. The Leviathan, roaring in pain, took two steps back and turned to head away from the fortress gates towards the ships. The naval fleet, seeing the threat, turned to deliver a broadside. The metal ship had vanished. Daniel pointed at the giant which was now wading towards the fleet.

"It's going to attack our allies!"

Captain Crimson shook her head.

"That changes nothing. We'll keep to our plan."

Despite her confident response, Captain Crimson started to walk towards the edge of the hill and the fortress. Her voice was shaky as she waved them forward.

"Come on, then. Let's get going."

As they climbed towards the brow of the hill, Daniel saw more and more of the fortress below. Giant iron walls shielded towering chimneys, black smoke flowing into the sky like blood into water; huge cylindrical boilers stood towards the back of the fortress, mammoth pipes leading into them from the mountainside. The smell of burning stung his throat and eyes as he looked towards the gate and saw, closer now, the defenders on the wall. Their metal body parts glinted in the sun, flashing like the fire from the muskets and cannons which shot at the ship trapped in the harbour below. Daniel tried to see what was happening down there but the rising brow of the hill hid the ship itself; only the tall masts and topsails could now be seen. Out beyond the walls, the Leviathan was tearing into the naval fleet; HMS Oppressive was already sinking, the stern punched into driftwood by the claws of the monster. Only the Admiral's skill kept the rest of the fleet alive; at his command, two ships tacked and gybed against the wind, coming about to fire at the back of the beast's legs. As it turned to swat at them, HMS Cantankerous swept past the great beast's ankles, slowing long enough to rescue several men from the sea and unleash a close range volley at the giant. It was a daring move; Daniel could see the Admiral standing high on the poop deck, shouting orders. The situation was urgent, Daniel knew.

"You aren't suggesting we climb down there?"

Rolf Fleppa's voice caused Daniel to glance back. They had reached the brow of the hill. Daniel gasped; in front of them stood a steep cliff, like a crater's edge. It fell away sharply to the fortress below. Now the ship was visible in the fortress harbour; the flash of red moving on the deck where the fake Captain Crimson fought for his life and the lives of his crew. Several fires were burning on the deck and a few Iron Pirates had boarded, and were fighting with the crew. The real Captain Crimson spoke, answering the Wizard's question.

"No, I'm not suggesting that we climb down there."

A look of relief crossed Rolf Fleppa's face. Daniel hated him in that moment for his cowardice. The look soon faded as Captain Crimson spoke again.

"I'm commanding that we climb down there. Move."

The climb was risky, even more so as it was done at speed. Several times Daniel slipped and he was not alone; only a combination of luck and good reflexes kept them from falling to their deaths among the rocks and steel below as the rain made the ground slippery and stung their eyes. Occasional flashes of cannon fire and booms of explosive thunder caused them to flinch; Daniel was certain that they would be spotted and shot from the wall but everyone was too busy with the battle to notice them. Their destination, it seemed, wasn't the ship and the battle; it was a steel shed at the back of the fortress, where the pipes from the mountain entered through the wall. As he climbed downwards, Daniel noticed a trapdoor hidden amongst the rocks and rubble. He called out to Captain Crimson, who was climbing a few feet to his left.

"There's a trapdoor."

She winked at him.

"Very observant, lad. There's a trapdoor and we're going into it."

Daniel glanced down again.

"Are you going to tell me what our plan is yet?"

"No."

Another explosion resonated through the cliff face. They kept climbing.

Rolf Fleppa was the last to arrive. His slow climbing irritated everyone; he couldn't help it, but with the battle raging and people dying while they stood and waited, it was hard not to be annoyed. Eventually, he jumped down the last few feet, landing with an exaggerated groan.

"I think I've injured my legs. I need to rest for a minute."

Captain Crimson pulled open the trapdoor with an agonising scream of metal on metal.

"You can rest for as long as it takes us all to climb in; if you fall behind after that, you're on your own."

Underneath the trapdoor was a shaft downwards; a metal ladder attached to the side of the shaft disappeared into the gloom. Captain Crimson was first in. She swung herself into position and climbed down with ease. Daniel jumped in next and scuttled down as fast as he was able; the shaft was only short and the climb took a few seconds. He found Captain Crimson at the bottom, lighting a torch; they were at the end of a rocky passage. Daniel seized the moment.

"If we're about to risk our lives for your plan, I think we deserve to know what it is. After all, if we don't know, we can't help if you get killed or injured."

Captain Crimson put her coat and hat on.

"Very well. Once the others arrive, I'll tell you."

She started the explanation before Rolf Fleppa arrived.

"So, the plan, gentlemen. I'll explain as we walk. Try to keep up."

She set off, walking into the rocky darkness of the tunnel, talking as she went.

"You all know that Captain Ironskull powers his ship with fire and steam?"

There were murmurs from the others. Captain Crimson carried on.

"We don't know how he does it, but we're sure that he has somehow tapped into the power of this mountain to help him. That's what those pipes coming out of the mountain are for. We also believe that the place where he controls this power from is normally well guarded. This is why we have attacked the front gate with all our ships; to make sure all of his Iron Pirates joined in the fight."

Daniel interrupted.

"Is that why you needed someone else to look like you?"

Captain Crimson threw him a look, but answered anyway.

"Yes. I needed him to believe that I was out there, on board my ship. Anything that made him suspicious about the attack could spoil our plan."

Owen also called out from near the back of the group.

"So what is the plan?"

"Patience! You're a hasty young gallowmonkey who needs to learn respect for his betters!"

There was a second or two of silence before Skop Groggen picked up where Captain Crimson had left off.

"The plan is for us to break into his fortress and make his steam boilers explode."

Captain Crimson started again.

"Yes. If everyone is fighting at the front, they won't see us sneak in at the back until it's too late. Remember; we need to destroy those boilers."

Daniel spoke up again, with one more question.

"How will we get out again before it all explodes?"

Skop Groggen answered in a quiet voice.

"We don't know."

They strode on through the darkness. No more words were said, the only sound was the occasional distant explosion, rumbling through the rock. Time passed; it could have been a minute or an hour. Only the flickering shadows and tramping of boots reminded Daniel that he was alive, that he hadn't already been swallowed by unending darkness. He fought against the fear that threatened to take control of him; part of him wanted the journey to end, part of him wanted it to go on forever. Just when he thought that the journey might never end, an iron door loomed out of the dark, a metal wheel stuck to the front. It reminded Daniel of a safe.

"Here we are. Everyone ready?"

Captain Crimson's voice was far too cheerful for the circumstances. Skop Groggen slipped past Daniel to stand by the door. He turned and addressed the small group in a low voice.

"Right, you all know the plan now. Behind this door is the main control and boiler room; in here, heat from the mountain boils water for steam. That steam powers the whole fortress and the Iron Ship; we don't know how it works but that doesn't matter. We do know that without the steam, the ship and fortress are totally powerless."

He paused. Nobody laughed at the joke so he carried on.

"We don't know what is behind this door; we expect a few guards. Your job is to fight them off while I overload the boilers. Then we fight our way out to the front of the fortress."

Own raised a shaky hand. Captain Crimson motioned towards him.

"Yes?"

"Why don't we go back through the tunnel?"

Captain Crimson answered.

"Two reasons. Firstly, it will be full of fire as soon as the boiler explodes. Secondly, I want to stand face to face with Captain Ironskull when he is defeated and look him in his cold mechanical eyes. Now come on, let's go."

Swords were drawn with a quiet hiss. Skop Groggen turned the wheel. With a hiss and a cloud of steam, the door swung open.

They charged through the door with a roar. The room behind was large, with metal walls and a high ceiling, where metal gave way to rock. Most of the room was dominated by a giant brass dome atop a huge cylinder. Steam issued from the joints of several pipes running into and out of the dome, while brass dials and wheels covered the front. The whole room was lit by a red glow from the fire within, shown through a circular glass window in the front. However, it wasn't the boiler that drew their attention. It was Captain

Ironskull and his fifty Iron Pirates who stood inside the door, weapons drawn. The roar died on the small party's lips as their charge stopped, shock on their faces. Captain Ironskull grinned.

"Well, well. Captain Crimson. I've been expecting you."

Chapter 14: The Traitor and the Hero

Steam pistols, flintlocks, and swords aimed at the small band, pinning them against the wall. Captain Crimson took her hat off and swept it in front of her in a deep bow.

"Well now, Captain Ironskull. It seems that you've beaten us to the punch and I take my hat off to you. Care to tell us how you knew we were coming?"

Captain Ironskull stepped forward. His arm housed a massive steam powered cannon with six barrels, which rotated with a low mechanical whine. He kept it levelled towards Captain Crimson.

"Why don't I send you all to your graves without explaining anything?"

Skop Groggen stepped forwards.

"I don't think you'll do that. If you just wanted us dead, you'd just have sunk us on our way in, or shot us all with your mechanical cannon as we walked in. There's a reason you built a gate to trap us and set an ambush for us here. Why don't you tell us what's really going on?"

Captain Ironskull laughed, a cruel metallic sound.

"Put your weapons down, they aren't going anywhere."

His crew responded, lowering their weapons but keeping them in hand. Captain Ironskull gestured towards Skop Groggen.

"This one speaks truly. I do want you alive; some of you at least. Men, bring them with me."

They were led out through an airlock style door, with rust creeping outwards from each rivet, then along a damp corridor with walls of rock and iron. Occasional drips of water plopped onto their heads; each prisoner was accompanied by a huge Iron Pirate. None dared to resist; all hoped that an opportunity to escape might appear later. It was a very faint hope which faded with every ringing metallic footstep.

They emerged from a gateway which was stained brown by the dripping of rusty water, each shielding their eyes as the dull glow of the Iron Fortress gave way to the lightning of the storm. They were at the harbour side, close to the imprisoned ship; flashes of gunfire still flickered between the Iron Pirates swarming along the harbour onto the deck and the crew at the bow of the ship. The fight was as good as over; only a handful were still fighting and more Iron Pirates arrived by the second. Most of the crew were tied up at the stern, the red coat of the fake Captain Crimson visible among them on the deck, the massive form of Boulder now obvious despite the disguise. The real Captain Crimson gave away a flash of emotion for the first time since their capture.

"Captain Ironskull, they're beaten men. Let them live. Your fight's with me."

Captain Ironskull laughed.

"Some may live, some may die. I care not either way. It is you I want, Captain Crimson; now you will see why."

They were marched away from the ship, towards the main gate of the fortress. Glancing right, Daniel saw the massive silhouette of the Leviathan raging in the shallow sea outside. He tried to share a look with George or even Owen but both had their heads down and the Iron Pirate guarding him pushed Daniel's head forward to face the front of the fortress. The huge gate opened with a rumble of moving chains, sliding upwards with a smooth motion and a smell of heated oil. The chamber behind was vast and full of steam, heat and red light; forward they were taken, into that cavernous hell.

The room was dominated by giant tanks of boiling red liquid. Huge metal tubes fed them, coming straight in from the mountain which formed the back of the cavern. In front of the tanks stood several steel coffins, each man sized with tubes and wires attached to the sides and brass dials on the front. A single tube led from the boiling red vats to a box above the coffins, feeding the liquid down towards them. Captain Ironskull marched ahead to stand in front of the coffins, then turned to face them. As he did so, the procession halted.

"Now you see, Captain Crimson. Here is why I want you alive."

With a sweep of his mechanical gun arm, he gestured towards the whole terrifying setup. Daniel felt sick with fear. Captain Crimson kept her chin high.

"What is this? Your kitchen? You want me alive so I can cook your dinner and wash your dishes?"

It was a poor joke and nobody laughed. Captain Ironskull walked to face Captain Crimson with steps so slow it was painful. He paused in front of her.

"Ability and cunning such as yours is too great a prize to waste. Far from killing you, I offer you a great gift; you, and those of your crew who are worth keeping. Together, we can rule the seas."

Captain Crimson snorted.

"There's a problem there. I'm a pirate captain, and we aren't good at taking orders. There's no way I'd sail under your flag anyway, you rusty bilge pot. Now, are you going to tell us how you knew we were coming through your back door? Does your technology give you mind reading powers?"

Captain Ironskull smiled.

"No. It was far simpler than that. I was told of your plans by one of your own men."

"Never! None of my men would betray us!"

The fury in Captain Crimson's voice was swiftly dispelled as Captain Ironskull gestured at the line of prisoners.

"One certainly would. Not only that, he is here among you. I wonder if he has the courage to step forward?"

Everyone looked along the line; Daniel saw Rolf Fleppa looking at him with questioning eyes. Fighting his anger at the unspoken suspicion that he could be the traitor, he glanced towards Owen. The former bully looked down at the floor. Captain Crimson and Skop Groggen kept their gaze forward. Captain Ironskull extended an arm.

"Don't be afraid. Step forward. Receive the reward I promised."

Daniel looked sideways to see if anyone would dare to move. He looked at Owen again, who glanced back at him with a defiant glare.

George stepped forward.

"You! Why?"

Daniel found himself shouting at his friend in shock and disbelief. Owen's mouth dropped open in surprise. Captain Crimson spat on the floor.

"The Admiral's man has sold us out. His man is the traitor, yet he dares to call us pirates dishonest."

Captain Ironskull laughed.

"This young man has wisdom beyond his years. He sees where the power will be in the future. Your days of wood, wind and wizardry are ending. Steam and iron, fire and brass are the future; mechanical power will take the place of wind, wood and superstition. The lad knows this and will be rewarded with his place among my officers."

George faced Captain Ironskull. Everyone shouted at once until Captain Ironskull blasted his machine gun arm into the air.

"There is no need to yell."

His tone turned calm as he continued;

"I understand your anger; change is hard to understand and harder still to accept. However, I will make each of you the same offer I made this man; join me. These machines will add living metal to your weak flesh, making you as I am. Together, we will rule the seas."

Skop Groggen looked at the machines, then back at Captain Ironskull.

"You have a whole crew of Iron Pirates already. Why bother with us?"

Captain Ironskull looked at each of them in turn.

"Whenever you make new discoveries, the early versions of what you create are always weaker than the later versions. My Iron Pirates are powerful but the change has robbed them of much of their intelligence."

Captain Crimson snorted.

"Can't say I noticed."

Captain Ironskull ignored her.

"I have rebuilt my machines, as you can see; my new Iron Pirates will keep their minds and their intelligence, if the machines work as they should. This is my offer; become my new crew. Join me, or die!"

Captain Crimson spat towards Captain Ironskull.

"That's a simple choice. I'd much rather die than be one of your crew."

Captain Ironskull shook his head sadly.

"That is a shame. I had hoped you would see reason but you leave me no choice."

Gesturing towards the others, Captain Ironskull pronounced his judgement.

"Kill them all, and those on the ship."

"What?"

Captain Crimson struggled but she was held firmly by her guards.

"You said you needed a new crew; why kill them? It makes no sense!"

Captain Ironskull sneered his reply.

"Yes. I also said that you were the one I wanted, and that I didn't care if the others lived or died. You, on the other hand, seem to want them alive. So, here is my new offer; agree to sail with me or I kill every one of them."

He paused for a second, then added;

"Slowly. And I'll make you watch them suffer."

Captain Crimson paused for a few seconds, clearly torn.

"Don't give in to him!"

Skop Groggen's cry was meant to strengthen Captain Crimson's resolve but it had the opposite effect. She slumped, beaten.

"Ok, Captain Ironskull. You win. You'd better hope my mind is destroyed though, because if I have any free will left, I'm never going to be loyal to you."

Captain Ironskull motioned towards the coffin in the middle.

"Strap her in."

The guards started to lead Captain Crimson forward. Owen yelled as he thrashed against his guards.

"Stop! Take me instead!"

Captain Ironskull stopped his guards with a wave.

"So. You want to be a hero and take the place of your captain, do you? Tell me; why should I accept that offer?"

Owen kept his gaze firm.

"You haven't used your new equipment, have you?"

"So?"

Owen continued.

"So, if it goes wrong you'll lose Captain Crimson, or her mind at least. Test it on me instead. If it works, I'll be the first of your new crew. If it fails, I'm just like your other mindless metal men. Either way, it's better than being killed."

Captain Ironskull nodded.

"This man has convinced me. For his bravery, he will have his place among my crew. Strap him in."

Owen was led forward. A few steps before the equipment, he paused.

"Let me walk the last few paces on my own, please."

The guard relaxed his grip on Owen's arms. Owen took three nervous steps forward, his hands reaching out to touch the cold iron of the lid as it stood, propped against the side of the coffin. He gripped it in two hands, holding it as if examining it, to see what it was. Captain Ironskull grew impatient.

"Hurry up. Put him in."

The Iron Pirate stepped forward. Owen turned round and smashed him in the face with the coffin lid, sending him sprawling.

"Shoot him!"

Captain Ironskull shouted at the rest of the Iron Pirates. All raised their guns but before they could fire, Owen spun around, holding the lid in front of him like a shield. Gunfire echoed around the cavern but the shots pinged off the lid, leaving Owen unharmed.

"Wait; stop shooting. We mustn't damage the equipment. I'll deal with him myself."

Captain Ironskull strode forward but Owen turned away and threw the lid as hard as he could into the huge tube above the coffins. The tube split open as the lid sliced into it, the edge acting like a blade. It wasn't completely sliced in two but the gash was large enough that steam and red liquid burst out, gushing down onto the equipment which exploded with a blast of fire. Owen was flung backwards as the blast destroyed everything. A wailing siren began to sound as boiling liquid pumped from the ragged end of the tube, flowing across the floor like blood from a wound.

"You fool! What have you done?"

Captain Ironskull charged forward to where Owen lay. Crawling to his knees, Owen looked up at him.

"I've stopped you."

Captain Ironskull picked up Owen with one hand. Lifting him high into the air, he hurled him into the remains of the ruined equipment, which collapsed into a pile of melting junk. Daniel looked in horror at the broken body of Owen, lying among the wreckage of the machines. He could barely see for the steam, which was now filling the room like a thick fog. Iron Pirates rushed about in panic; Captain Ironskull just stood and stared at his ruined machines. Daniel didn't know what to feel; Owen had made his life miserable for years but what he had just done was brave beyond words and had possibly saved their lives. Before he could spend too long thinking about it, Skop Groggen grabbed his arm and pulled him away.

"Time to leave."

Chapter 15: The end of the war

There was chaos all around. Fire and steel merged together in a terrible inferno as the cavern fell apart around the escaping pirates. On the harbourside, things were little better. Prisoners were escaping from the ship as Iron Pirates ran back and forth in panic; Daniel soon realised why. With the destruction of the main chamber of the fortress, the turrets had lost power and stopped firing. Above them, lightning lit up the terrible form of the Leviathan, its tendril covered head roaring as the giant fists smashed into the gate. Captain Crimson roared over the noise of the battle;

"To the ship! We must fight our way free!"

Kicking an Iron Pirate into the water, Skop Groggen somersaulted along the quay, landing on his feet.

"Follow me!"

He ran, the others following. The Iron Pirates tried to stop them but without their former discipline they were easily swept aside by Captain Crimson's desperate crew. Skop Groggen swiftly drew alongside the ship but ran past. Captain Crimson stopped and shouted.

"What are you doing? The ship is here!"

Skop Groggen paused, and grinned over his shoulder.

"Yes, I see it. You set the rest of the crew free and make sure those boilers are destroyed, I've got something else to do."

Daniel was next in line behind Skop Groggen. The wizard turned to him.

"You, boy. Come with me. I'll need a hand."

Skop Groggen jumped, spun and kicked his way past several more Iron Pirates, with Daniel running hard just to keep up. They ran to the end of the wall, where it met the cliff at the edge of the fortress. A steep set of steps led to a narrow walkway at the top of the wall and it was up these steps that Skop Groggen ran, bounding upwards two at a time. Daniel followed; the steps were covered with a thin layer of black slime and it was hard not to slip. Daniel glanced down; seeing the drop down to filthy water below, he slowed down and placed each foot with care. By the time he reached the top, Skop Groggen was almost at the closest tower.

Daniel balanced along the walkway. The wind blew in from the sea, spray stinging his face with each gust. Storm clouds loomed, darkening the sun and bringing rain which was falling in earnest, making the walkway even more treacherous. Ahead, Daniel could see the bounding form of Skop Groggen, dodging under the huge fists of the Leviathan as it smashed the tower and the gateway. The roar of the monster throbbed through his chest; the sheer size of the creature making the whole thing seem unbelievable. The great beast's shadow made the wall even darker as it loomed over them; it was only that they were so tiny compared to the Leviathan that kept it from crushing them both like ants. Daniel had no idea what the small wizard was trying to do or why he needed help but he swallowed his fear and ran on anyway, squinting against the spray and the rain.

Skop Groggen was sticking a fuse into a barrel of gunpowder as Daniel arrived.

"Quick, help me get this over the edge!"

The fuse was already sizzling. Not wanting to be near the Leviathan nor the barrel when the fuse ran out, Daniel pushed as hard as he could. There was a splash from far below and at that moment, the Leviathan spotted them; eyes of pure violence stared down at them. A huge fist raised to smash them out of existence but before it could hammer home the blow, an explosion from near its feet rocked the tower. Both Skop Groggen and Daniel were knocked onto their backs as the monster roared in anger and pain. It turned to swipe at the invisible hurt. As it did, Skop Groggen jumped to his feet.

"Quick, help me pile up the rest of the barrels."

"Why? What are you going to do?"

Skop Groggen grinned a dangerous grin.

"I'm going to let the Admiral know we're still alive, and make a hole for our ship to sail through. Oh, and get rid of the Leviathan while I'm at it."

Many barrels of gunpowder were already piled against the wall, next to the turret's giant cannon. With Daniel's help, Skop Groggen added the few that were left elsewhere to the pile. The wizard then turned to the young lad.

"Now, I'm going to ask you to do something extremely dangerous. Before the Leviathan starts to attack again; I need you to put a line of gunpowder from the pile of barrels to the edge of the turret."

Daniel nodded once.

"What will you do?"

"As soon as you finish, I'll light it. Then we both run. First, I have to do this."

Skop Groggen pulled a dead chicken from somewhere. Turning away, Daniel's hands trembled as he laid the trail of gunpowder. Behind him, Skop Groggen lit a small torch. The roar of the Leviathan grew louder once more as the monster loomed over the turret. The stink of dead fish filled the air like a cloud of disease. Daniel threw the last of the powder on the floor and ran. Dropping his torch onto the end of the trail, Skop Groggen threw the chicken over the wall and ran with him.

Daniel chanced a single look back as he ran along the wall top, and instantly wished he hadn't. A huge hand swung mere feet from him, knocking chunks of wall away, dangerously close to his feet. Stumbling forward, his foot slipped, sending him skidding sideways. His hand grabbed at the wet stones, slipping away, desperately seeking something to hold him up and finding only fresh air. Panic swept over him as he slid off the wall; he looked down through instinct and saw rock and seawater many feet below, a terrible place to land and a nasty way to die. A scream flew from his throat, pure terror in sound form.

A hand grabbed his hand.

Daniel swung in the air; Skop Groggen hauled him up onto the edge of the wall. Daniel was amazed by his strength. Skop Groggen had pulled him up with one arm. The familiar grin greeted him as he was hauled to safety.

"Don't go down there. That's a bad idea."

Daniel looked up at him from the wall.

"Thank you."

He intended to say more, but an enormous explosion threw them both into space and blew the consciousness from them in an instant.

Time passed; all around was noise and darkness. Daniel had no idea how long he was suspended in space, blind and helpless. He heard voices; great sorrow gripped his heart as Owen's voice drifted through his mind. At the same time, he heard the roar of battle, the clash of weapons and the screams of the dying. Drawn closer and closer to Owen's voice, the battle faded. Daniel's bedroom began to swim into focus.

Landing in cold water woke him up, the sudden shock of total immersion ripping him back to the world of the pirates. A gasped breath burned his lungs and brought a fresh wave of panic; choking to get the water out meant more gasped breaths, more burning in his lungs, more panic. Seconds that felt like hours passed; Daniel's arms and legs flailed uselessly. Eventually, his head broke the surface of the water. He coughed, bringing up water with each splutter. A massive shadow loomed across him; Daniel feared that it was the Leviathan but one look told him that it was the ship; the explosion had blasted him back into the harbour and by some miracle he had avoided death against the harbour wall and death against the side of the ship. A rope dropped into the water next to him. Daniel grabbed it with an arm of jelly. He tried to pull himself up but had no strength left. Instead, he wrapped the rope around his waist and was hauled aboard.

Daniel just lay motionless on the deck for a time. By the time he had the strength to stand up, the ship was sailing. Daniel saw that they had passed through a gap in the wall where the tower used to stand; behind it, the burning fortress was falling apart while above it, ominous rumblings and smoke came from the mountain of fire. There was no sign of the Leviathan. Standing on wobbly legs like a newborn foal, Daniel gripped the mast to keep himself upright. Skop Groggen was standing next to Captain Crimson at the Bow rail. Ahead of them were the remains of the naval fleet, sadly depleted; only three of the ships were still afloat. Only enough crew to keep the ship sailing remained on deck and all were busy about their tasks. Daniel spoke to nobody as he made his way to the captain and the wizard.

"Feeling any better, Tom?"

Captain Crimson's voice had an unusual note of kindness. Skop Groggen maintained his usual grin.

"This boy is strong. He's fine."

Captain Crimson placed a hand on his shoulder.

"You were very lucky. If you'd landed a few feet either way, you wouldn't be talking to us now."

Daniel nodded. He didn't want to discuss his own brush with death so he changed the subject.

"What's happened to Captain Ironskull?"

Skop Groggen answered.

"We left him behind, with his fortress falling down around his ears."

"You didn't capture him?"

Daniel realised that his question sounded like an accusation but Captain Crimson didn't seem to mind.

"We were busy fighting our way free; it was hard enough to get away without trying to take prisoners. Nobody wanted to run back into the burning remains of the fortress. We did pick up the traitor, though; the fight went out of him as soon as we pointed our flintlocks at his mutinous head."

Daniel's anger rose as he was reminded of George's treachery.

"Where is he?"

Skop Groggen gestured with his head.

"In the brig, with a handful of other prisoners. After we've spoken to the Admiral, we'll decide what to do with him."

George's betrayal had cost Owen his life. Until his act of bravery, Daniel had hated the bully but his friend's betrayal now made him feel sad about his former tormentor's end.

"Enemy ship to starboard!"

The lookout's yell caused a mass stampede to the starboard rail and pulled Daniel away from his melancholy thoughts. His weakened state meant that he reached the rail last. Captain Ironskull's ship was closing on them fast; Daniel heard the frantic sounds of the gun crews below preparing to fire. The bow turret turned to face them. Captain Crimson shouted above the noise of the crew.

"All hands, arm yourselves. Get as close as possible and prepare to repel boarders. Show no mercy: We need to hold them long enough for the Navy lads to get involved. Sell your lives dearly, lads! Take 'em with you into the abyss!"

Someone pressed a sword into Daniel's hand. Cannons roared from below them but the shots that hit were deflected from the metal hull. For some reason, the turret wasn't returning fire. This was puzzling until it turned to come alongside; no doubt preparing to capture Captain Crimson alive. Exhausted men prepared for one more fight as the hatches on the Iron Ship opened with a hiss of steam.

"Fire on my command!"

Captain Crimson shouted, arm held over her head. The first Iron Pirates emerged but they had their hands up in surrender.

"They're giving up!"

Captain Crimson looked sceptical.

"Careful lads, it could be a trap. Boulder, let them aboard one at a time. Tie each one up before the next comes aboard."

Before any of the Iron Pirates could cross to the ship, Captain Ironskull emerged. His mechanical hand now carried a small flagpole attachment, with a white flag attached. He walked to the front of his crew with none of his usual confidence.

"There's no trap, Captain Crimson. You've beaten us. Let me come aboard, I'm at your mercy."

Captain Ironskull was taken to the Admiral. The Admiral insisted on this, sending several officers to Captain Crimson's ship to demand handover of the prisoners as soon as he could see that they had been captured. The Admiral walked around his prisoner, who was tied to the mast of HMS Cantankerous.

"So. We have the lethal Captain Ironskull at last. Do you care to tell us why you chose to submit so easily? You know that you face the gallows."

Captain Ironskull looked down, his metal head reflecting the sunlight and contrasting with his miserable appearance.

"I would like nothing more than to fight on, and take out your pathetic wooden boats. The truth is, I can't. You've destroyed my fortress and with it, my source of power."

The Admiral stopped in front of the prisoner.

"Your source of power? Explain yourself."

Skop Groggen exchanged a look with Captain Crimson as Captain Ironskull replied.

"My fortress was built to harness the power of Fire Mountain."

Behind him, the volcano rumbled, as if the sound of it's name had drawn it's attention.

"With that power, we had enough steam to power the ship; once I discovered how to contain the power of the mountain inside the ship itself, I was invincible."

Captain Crimson smirked.

"Really? If you were invincible, why are you giving up?"

Looking at the faces of the naval officers and pirates, Captain Ironskull regained a little of his former arrogance.

"You know it's true. None of you could beat me until your lad's lucky throw destroyed my fortress."

Captain Crimson stepped forward.

"That, my metal headed nemesis, is where your arrogance was your undoing. You believed that we would be drawn in by your power and let us too close. That lad's bravery was your undoing. It cost you everything."

Captain Ironskull's head snapped up.

"You should've taken my offer, Captain Crimson. We could've ruled the seas. Now you've given all the power back to the navy, and to that pompous tyrant. You could've had everything but now we've both lost it all."

Captain Crimson replied in her most respectable voice.

"Not me. I'm an honest trader from now on."

She winked at Daniel The Admiral missed the gesture. His focus was on Captain Ironskull.

"Captain Crimson has been offered a full pardon for any previous activity, in return for her assistance in bringing you to justice."

Captain Ironskull shook his head.

"If you believe that, you're more stupid than I thought. It won't matter soon anyway."

The Admiral raised an eyebrow.

"Care to tell us why?"

Captain Ironskull looked towards the island, the burning remains of his fortress and the rumbling volcano. He grinned an evil grin.

"Fire Mountain will kill you all."

Chapter 16: The last chapter

The rumble of Fire Mountain made them all look round. The Admiral fired a question into the air.

"Why should we fear the mountain now?"

Captain Ironskull sneered his reply.

"My fortress was drawing on the power of the mountain, as I told you. That power has to go somewhere and now my machines aren't using it, it's all going to come out through the mountainside."

For the first time Daniel could remember, Skop Groggen looked worried.

"Sir, I suggest we put that mountain to our stern and make sail with all haste."

The Admiral stood tall, his head high.

"We shall first secure all of the prisoners, Mr Church. It will not do to allow them to escape our custody."

An enormous explosion from the mountain ripped through the air, sending vast flaming chunks of stone flying towards them. Captain Crimson spoke over the sound of the explosion.

"With every respect, your Admiralty, we don't have time for that. If that mountain explodes, it won't matter which of us are prisoners and which are free men as we sink to the bottom as burned corpses."

The Admiral was torn. As the first lumps of stone hit the water, he stood, looking back and forth from Captain Ironskull to his men. Captain Ironskull siezed the moment; using his superhuman mechanical strength, he burst his ropes and walked towards his ship with a slow, determined tread. The Admiral pointed towards him and opened his mouth to shout but Skop Groggen laid a hand on his shoulder.

"It won't matter how many prisoners we have if all of us are dead, sir."

The Admiral made the only decision he could; they fled. Every sailor aboard every ship ran to his station and worked as if his life depended on it, which it did. Captain Ironskull climbed down to his ship as the Admiral and Captain Crimson ran around, shouting orders. Huge chunks of rock hit the water, sending hot spray across the decks; Fire Mountain was dying, and it seemed it wanted to take them all with it.

"I want every sail bulging now! Take off your shirts and breeches if you have to and tie them to the rigging, we need to be far away when that mountain goes bang!"

Captain Crimson's voice carried over the chaos and thunder. Daniel, unsure what to do, ran to the rail and looked back at the island. At least he could yell if they were about to be hit. Glancing across at the Iron Pirates, Daniel saw that Captain Ironskull was now standing, arms out to his sides, facing towards the island. He made no attempt to escape, he and his Iron Pirates looked like men who were awaiting the end of the world.

They sailed away as soon as they were able. The rain of fire had smashed the stern of one ship to matchwood; those who couldn't get into the lifeboats swam like madmen towards the other ships. The waves started to grow in size; the lifeboats danced about in the water like corks.

"Quickly, throw them ropes; we'll tow them away with us."

Captain Crimson's shout was met with a mumbled response from Boulder;

"They'll slow us down. We'll sink too."

Captain Crimson silenced him with a look. Nobody spoke another word as the ropes were thrown.

They sailed hard; Daniel stood at the aft rail, eyes fixed as the island destroyed itself in a blaze of devastation. As he watched, a block of stone fell like a dying comet into the Iron Ship, smashing it in two; it was as if the mountain was taking revenge on the Iron Pirates. Daniel looked but there was no sign of Captain Ironskull. The last thing he saw of the ship was the two halves sinking below the waves.

"She's going to blow!"

The cry came from a naval officer; seconds later, the mountain gave it's last blast; a huge explosion which shot hundreds of tons of flaming rocky death into the air. Daniel watched as the hail of doom flew towards them with a terrifying inevitability. The first few splashed harmlessly into the water. Then he saw the wave.

"Tie yourselves down boys! Our only hope is that we don't capsize when that wave hits!"

Captain Crimson was already lashing herself to the wheel as she saw the wave and shouted the order. The crew looked towards the island; a wave which was twice as high as the ship was coming towards them; to Daniel, it looked like a wall of water. Skop Groggen had grabbed some rope. As if stung, the rest of the crew stopped staring and ran to grab whatever lengths of rope they could.

Daniel managed to grab a piece of rope from a loose sail. The roar of the approaching wave was unmistakeable as he wrapped the length of it around himself. Racking his brains, Daniel tried to remember any of the knots he had learned as a cub scout. In the end, his trembling hands made do with a Granny knot as he braced himself for impact. His knuckles were white as he gripped the rope and the ship's rail. The ship bucked and weaved like a horse trying to throw her rider, before the water crashed down on them all. Daniel was smashed into unconsciousness again as the wave broke over their ship.

He awoke in his bedroom. Owen was sitting on the bed, looking pale but very much alive. Daniel had never been so pleased to see him. George was still lying on the floor. Owen greeted Daniel with a nod as he awoke and sat up. He gestured towards the prone form of George.

"What do we do with him?"

Before an answer could be given, George groaned and sat up. Owen stood and loomed over him.

"Get up, traitor."

Owen grabbed George's collar and hauled him to his feet. Spinning him around on wobbly legs, Owen pinned George up to the wall with a hand around his throat. George tried to protest his innocence but Owen's grip was causing him to splutter. Daniel called out to him;

"Let him go, Owen. He's the one who has to live with what he did, nothing you do will change that for better or worse."

Surprisingly, Owen let go. Like a cat released from a cage, George ran out of the room. They heard the front door slam as he left the house.

There was a silence that seemed to last forever. Owen broke it.

"Don't think this makes us friends."

Daniel nodded.

"No. We'll never be that."

Owen looked at him, as if noticing him properly for the first time.

"I'll leave you alone from now on, though. I'll make sure the others give you no trouble as long as you don't give us a reason."

Daniel allowed himself a small smile.

"I won't give you a reason, trust me."

Daniel paused again, before speaking to his old adversary.

"Thank you."

Owen looked puzzled.

"What for?"

"You saved my life and got yourself killed doing it. That was real bravery you showed back there."

For the first time ever, Owen looked embarrassed.

"Well, it just seemed like the right thing to do. Anyway, I'm still alive here."

He paused.

"If you ever tell anyone, I'll tell them you made it all up. It never happened, understand?"

Owen left shortly after that. Daniel, exhausted as he was, needed to find out what happened to the ships. He had been knocked out, he knew that much but if Owen had been killed and yet woken up in their own world, could the same have happened to him? Had the ships been destroyed by the falling rocks and the wave? Had anyone survived? Picking up the book, Daniel found the page as fast as he could.

The Admiral stood like a figurehead on the bow of the lifeboat, his head held high as his men pulled hard on the oars. Boulder looked down at him from the aft rail.

"Looks like he rules the world. Cocky old..."

Captain Crimson cut him off.

"The Admiral knows full well that he owes us. It may be pure luck that the Crimson Firedrake was the only survivor of the fire and the wave but we could just as easily have left him and his men sitting in their lifeboats, alone on the sea. He may look like a conquering lord but it must be killing him to have to be towed along by us. I'm just hoping that he'll crack before we get to port and beg me to let him aboard the ship."

Skop Groggen, walking up behind them, joined in the conversation before either knew he was there.

"You know he won't. He'll order you to give him command of the vessel and if you refuse, he'll threaten to withdraw your pardon."

Captain Crimson sighed.

"You could at least let me dream of humiliating him for a bit longer before you pour cold water on my fantasy. Come on, I need some rum."

With that, Captain Crimson left the rail and strode away across the deck.

Daniel closed the book. He realised that he'd been holding his breath; he let it out with a long sigh. A tiredness he hadn't known was there flooded over him, accompanied by the relief of reading that his friends had survived. Unable to fight it off, Daniel fell asleep.

The next day, Daniel passed Owen, Barry and Bill by the school gate. The familiar lurch of fear in his stomach rose up as he walked by. However, Barry and Bill ignored him. For a brief moment, he made eye contact with Owen; his look was greeted with a tiny nod, so small that only Daniel noticed it. It was enough. He walked on through the gate free of fear for the first time in as long as he could remember.

He sat next to George in the first lesson of the day. It was a science lesson; they were split into pairs to work on an experiment. The first few minutes were spent in painful silence as George avoided Daniel, spending the time collecting the equipment. Eventually, Daniel managed to talk to him when the teacher told him to sit down and get on with his work. He wasted no time, getting straight to the point.

"Are you going to tell me why you did it?"

George looked down at the table.

"I had no choice."

"You always have a choice."

Daniel was in no mood to let him off easily. George carried on, miserably.

"It was Captain Ironskull. He grabbed me on the boat that day, he said that I had to spy for him or he would kill me. He'd just killed all the other men. What could I do?"

Daniel snarled his reply.

"You could've told me, once we got back. We could've sorted it out together. Instead, you went behind my back, used my map without asking and betrayed us, right when we needed you the most."

"I'm sorry."

"You're a coward."

A long pause followed this accusation. Daniel knew how much his words must hurt his friend, but at that moment he didn't care. Eventually, George looked up.

"We're still friends, aren't we?"

Daniel left a long pause again. He remembered how horrible it felt to be the outcast. Looking at his friend, he saw a boy at his mercy; he could crush him, as others had done to him, or he could choose to do something different. George's actions had hurt him but he was his friend after all; when he did reply, it was with a sigh.

"Yes. We're still friends. You've got some work to do to prove I can trust you though."

George nodded.

"I know."

George spent the rest of the lesson being a bit too helpful to Daniel; offering to do all the writing, clearing up after the experiment, even offering to buy him a drink at break time. In the end, Daniel had to tell him to stop it. He also put George off following him home by declaring that he had to take the book back to his Uncle Alexander. This was true; he had planned to take the book back after school but it was also a good reason to get away from his friend. By the end of the afternoon, Daniel just wanted to be alone and he left the final Maths lesson as if the class was on fire.

His uncle was waiting in the back room of the shop when he arrived.

"Enjoyed it, did you?"

Daniel handed the book and map over.

"I did. I'm going to miss it. Some books are so good, it feels like you've lost friends when you finish them."

Uncle Alexander laughed.

"This one more than most, I expect."

Daniel nodded.

"Yes, this one more than most. I was pleased that the main characters didn't die."

His uncle raised an eyebrow.

"I believe Captain Ironskull went down with his ship."

Daniel shrugged.

"You know what I mean. Anyway, how do you know about that?"

Uncle Alexander didn't answer, instead he walked across to pick up two freshly brewed cups of tea. As he set them on the table, he pushed the map back towards Daniel.

"I think you'll need this more than me."

Daniel looked up at him, puzzled.

"Why?"

Uncle Alexander gestured towards the shelf behind him, where a stack of old books lay, undisturbed.

"I have another book for you to borrow. Call it a sequel, if you like. Your next adventure awaits you, Daniel…"

43417017R00067

Made in the USA
Charleston, SC
27 June 2015